"You don't know me from Adam!"

Kyle lashed out at her coldly. "I'm about to introduce myself!"

His arm came around Alexandra's waist and their bodies touched. He laced his fingers through her hair and his strong hand cradled her head as he gathered her close.

The kiss shattered her. It was timeless, brief, but unending. For seconds she lost all sense of reality as a curtain of stars seemed to come down and enclose them both.

It seemed a long time before she could speak, and all the time his gray eyes watched her, his face expressionless.

"You—you had no right to do that," she whispered. "It was..."

"Wicked? Insensitive? Unforgivable?" he inquired helpfully, disdain on his face. "For a few seconds, Alexandra, you were mindless."

PATRICIA WILSON used to live in Yorkshire, England, but with her children all grown up, she decided to give up her teaching position there and accompany her husband on an extended trip to Spain. Their travels are providing her with plenty of inspiration for her romance writing.

Books by Patricia Wilson

HARLEQUIN PRESENTS

HARLEQUIN ROMANCE

PATRICIA WILSON

curtain of stars

Harlequin Books

TORONTO • NEW YORK • LONDON
AMSTERDAM • PARIS • SYDNEY • HAMBURG
STOCKHOLM • ATHENS • TOKYO • MILAN
MADRID • WARSAW • BUDAPEST • AUCKLAND

Harlequin Presents first edition April 1992
ISBN 0-373-11454-0

Original hardcover edition published in 1990
by Mills & Boon Limited

CURTAIN OF STARS

CHAPTER ONE

ALEXANDRA went along to the staff meeting feeling sub-
limely confident. Gerald Norton, the general manager
of Fosdick-Kent Plastics, had called an 'emergency
meeting'. The only emergency about it was his own panic,
as Alexandra knew quite well. He was in a flat spin and
wanted company, but she felt that it hardly concerned
her. If the firm was closed down she wouldn't have to
face Gerald Norton again, for one thing.

He looked irritably round as everyone squeezed themselves into his office, and his looks were sufficiently grim
to bring a quick silence. 'Well, he's won! He's taken
over and he'll be here tomorrow. We're about to be
stripped to the bone!'

He looked at his captive audience and saw the pre-
dictable gloom. He had summoned them here to impart
gloomy information, and their expressions were
satisfyingly despondent. They were in shark-infested
waters now, his tight voice made that plain. Stripped to
the bone. There wasn't a person present who could feel
secure. The whole of the staff of the London office
expected to be redundant forthwith.

'I can't see any reason to panic,' Alexandra announced firmly. 'This is purely a business take-over. It
happens all the time. These things are normally just paper
transactions.'

Gerald Norton turned on her irascibly. 'For heaven's
sake, Alex! Haven't you been listening to anything I've
said for the past few months? This is no ordinary take-
over. There's nothing wrong with this company, nothing

5

weak. Kyle Maddison has made millions by doing exactly what he intends to do to us now. He's an asset-stripper! Now he's got control he'll take us apart. Every single paying part will be singled out and sold. Every part that's flagging will be scrapped, regardless of who works there. He's utterly ruthless. Even if I hadn't told you, you could have found that out by watching his manoeuvres. At the beginning not one single shareholder was going to sell—now look. He's got fifty-five per cent of the company.'

'Apparently he's charming.'

The little feminine remark from one of the staff turned Gerald's face deep red.

'So is a tiger, when it's caged,' he grated. 'Don't imagine that feminine wiles will help at all—he's not short of females.' He turned to Alexandra, apparently sure that her remarks had set the stage for mutiny. 'And don't think your name will save you! Being called Kent will do you no good at all. He won't need a private secretary either—he'll bring his own team to dismantle us. He won't need any of us when the company's split up and the padlocks are on the doors. Did you sell your shares?' he asked truculently.

'I wasn't asked.' Alexandra felt highly amused, gleeful to see Gerald Norton in this anxious and bad-tempered state. The oily charm had quite disappeared. 'Nobody is at all interested in the few shares that Uncle Bob left Stevie and me. Kyle Maddison didn't want Stevie's either.'

'He's probably wary of the name. He'll take a close look at you and then ask for them as a gift,' Gerald said nastily.

'If you've quite finished, I'll go.' Alexandra stood and looked at him levelly. Tall and slim, her fair hair a cloud of shimmering silk that reached her shoulders, she let her dark eyes, almost purple-black, hold his fearlessly. He was a bully, and her contemptuous looks said it all.

'Don't forget that you still work here!' Backed into a corner, he snarled, the oily charm scraped bare.

'Only just, apparently. From what you've said I imagine he'll come crashing in here and take us to pieces. Caution seems to be unnecessary now.'

'He'll want my comments on the staff,' Gerald Norton warned in an ugly voice.

'You may be stripped to the bone with the rest of us,' Alexandra said sweetly as she walked out.

If he came after her and fired her on the spot she didn't care. She didn't care if the roof fell in. She had plenty to worry about that didn't even remotely concern the company and, as to her job, it was a relief to her that someone was taking over who just might get rid of Gerald Norton.

Since her Uncle Bob had died, Gerald Norton had been running the firm, his opinion of himself rising daily. He had immediately told her that she would be his own private secretary until things sorted themselves out, and it hadn't been long before she had been obliged to put him severely in his place. She had reminded him rather forcefully that he had a wife, and since then he had been particularly vicious, taking great pleasure in blocking every move she made. It had added pressure to her at work, just as she had pressure at home from Steven.

Yes, she hoped he got the push. She had no idea though what Kyle Maddison was really like. All she knew about him she had read in newspapers. Even yesterday there had been a full-page article about him. He was a business genius, a tycoon. Apparently everything he touched turned to gold. That seemed hardly likely if he gobbled everything up. It was probably only Gerald Norton's pique that he didn't have the power that apparently radiated from Kyle Maddison.

There were some people who said he was simply a raider. It made him sound just a bit like a pirate. He looked nothing like one, though; at least, his photograph in the newspaper hadn't looked like that. He had looked coldly handsome, aloof, quite above the sort of games that Gerald Norton liked to play. Still, you couldn't tell much from a newspaper photograph.

Eliot Davis caught up with her as she walked along to the lift. 'Don't let that creep worry you, Alex,' he said soothingly, stepping in with her and punching the button to the street level. 'He's in a wild panic.'

'Well, I hope it turns out that he has something to panic about,' Alexandra muttered. 'I hope Kyle Maddison takes one look at him and hands out his dismissal.'

'Not been bothering you again, has he?' Eliot asked crossly, but she shook her fair head decisively.

'Not likely! Not after the things I said. He just tries to make life uncomfortable, that's all.'

'Well, let me know if he gets to be too much.' The lift stopped and he took her arm gently. 'Dinner tonight?'

She was just going to say no, as she often did, but his way of coming out on her side every time deserved some reward and she smiled up at him. 'I'd love to.'

For a minute he couldn't quite believe it, but a grin spread across his pleasant face. 'Seven—I'll collect you from home. And let me know if you have any more trouble from the Big Creep.'

Alexandra nodded and stepped out into the foyer. It was nice to have support, but nobody could do anything about Gerald Norton, nobody except the new Wonder Man. Being chief accountant for the firm didn't give Eliot any power at all. No, it was all up to Kyle Maddison.

Alexandra knew that Steven was home as soon as she stopped her car outside the house. The music—if it could be called that—was deafening even out here, and their closest neighbour came to the door with a pained expression on her face.

'Alexandra! Really!'

'I know, Mrs Nash, I know. One minute and all will be peace and serenity.'

'Only while you're here, Alexandra. You'll have to do something about that brother of yours.'

'I will.'

Alexandra went inside the front door, almost reeling as the sound-waves hit her. Calling to him was useless. She marched up to his room, walked in and switched off the record-player.

'Alex! You've ruined the record. It cost me a fiver.'

'And you were robbed. It was ruined before it was ever produced. If I've asked you once I've asked you a thousand times not to play your records so loudly. The neighbours complain. They complain to *me*!'

'I'm sorry.'

He didn't look a bit contrite, and for a few seconds Alexandra glared at him. She couldn't keep it up, though. He was lounging on his bed, his face screwed up ruefully, his blond hair untidy, and instantly he was her baby brother again, even at seventeen. He did it on purpose, she was well aware of that, but he always got round her. When she looked at him she could still see how ill he had been when he had been younger. She had protected him then, and the instinct was still strong.

'How long have you been in?'

'About half an hour.' His expression altered subtly, but she swallowed her anxiety and smiled briskly.

'Right! Let's get tea ready. As you're here early you can help.'

He got up at once, and his expression was so relieved that she knew with a sinking heart he had been fired again. Two jobs in two months! He was hopeless, and she knew it. She hid her worries behind a smile and went down the stairs, her velvet dark eyes clouded as soon as her back was to him. It couldn't go on, but she had no idea how to stop it. It was her job to deal with people of all kinds, but she couldn't deal with her brother.

She was twenty-four, seven years older—it should have been easy. She was dealing with grown men every day, and here was a mere boy getting the better of her time after time. Of course, she didn't love the grown men— they were not all that remained of her family. It made a difference when it came to rational thought. Steven only had her now and she still watched for any signs of illness, although he had been better for years. Even so, he was ruining his life.

'What time do you start tomorrow?' She made the question as casual as she could as he helped to get tea ready.

'I don't. I'll be going to find another job in the morning.'

'I see.'

Instantly he was sulking and she turned to look at him, her eyes doing what they sometimes did now, seeing him clearly as a person and not as her baby brother. He was taller than she was. He had the family good looks, but he was utterly spoiled; she had simply continued what her parents had started, giving in to every whim he had in case he was back to being in bed each day. His hair was soon going to be as long as hers, too!

'I'm sick of working with idiots! I know more now than they've known in their lives.'

'This was a good place. The mechanics there are excellent. The boss used to drive Grand Prix cars.'

'Used to! He's about fifty!'

'Age overtakes us all.' Alexandra took the plates from him firmly. He was going to start banging things down soon, she could see it on his face.

'I could out-drive him *now*!'

'You lost your licence the week after you got it,' she reminded him. 'You also smashed my car up. That's not likely to get you to Le Mans.'

'There are no stupid restrictions on a track!'

'There's discipline,' Alexandra murmured.

He slammed the last plate down and walked to the door.

'What about your tea?' she asked wearily. They had been here before—many times.

'I don't want any! I'm going out at eight!'

He stamped upstairs and she listened carefully, her shoulders falling with relief as it became apparent that he was not yet defiant enough to turn the music up loudly again.

She had been just twenty-one when they had been left alone and it had been quite natural to let things continue as they had always been—essential, actually. Steven had succumbed to an attack of rheumatic fever when he had been ten years old and he had never seemed to get really better.

He was better now, or so medical experts had assured her, but he had always had his own way and by and large that was how the situation stood now. Any remonstrations and there was a scene, no matter how great had been his transgression. His only real interest was cars, and there was little doubt that he was some kind of mechanical genius—even at fifteen he had been able to strip a car apart and put it together again—but he had a contempt for others that was alarming and he saw no reason why he should not do exactly as he wished. His illness and the family's concern had left him with the idea that he should be first in everything. It was a state of affairs she had inherited, and the old dread of losing him was still there. He knew it too.

Alexandra was ironing when he appeared again, his face rueful.

'Sorry about the rage.'

He wasn't really. He just didn't like upsetting her, and that was something on the plus side. She smiled at him and ran an expert eye over his appearance. Hair too long but very clean. Was he smart? No, not to her liking. Steven made her feel old. He was grinning now at her surreptitious inspection, knowing that she disapproved of his 'gear', knowing too that she would not say a word.

'Take care. Will you be late in?'

She was voicing another worry. He stayed out until the early hours every night and, apart from the fact that it wasn't good for him, he had already been in serious trouble. He was still on probation. If he didn't find another job before too long...

'About twelve.' That was a lie and they both knew it. 'By the way,' he added with a quick change of subject, 'when will that new boss of yours take over?'

'Don't remind me! He's coming tomorrow. All we can hope is that he won't close us down. If he keeps the firm going he'll arrange things to his satisfaction and then put a manager in. He always does that. Until then we'll just have to grin and bear it. So long as he doesn't put Gerald Norton back in charge, everything will be fine.'

She had a feeling that everything wouldn't be fine, but it was pointless to discuss it with Steven. His interest was dying even now.

'You might come home engaged to him. He's rolling in money. Our worries would be over if he fancied you.'

'I wish I had your comfortably vague outlook on life,' Alexandra said crossly. 'I may be joining you when you go to look for a job.'

'No way! The name is Kent, remember? He's not going to fire the niece of the founder of the firm. Anyway, old Fosdick would have a stroke.'

'*Mr* Fosdick hasn't bothered with the firm for years!' Alexandra said in an annoyed voice. 'He's only kept

fifteen per cent of the shares and he's now sold out to
Kyle Maddison. Being called Kent won't do me any good
either. I'm hardly a major shareholder.'

That was a bit of a blow beneath the belt, she thought
guiltily as he had the grace to blush, but his rather pained
expression didn't last. He simply changed the subject
again.

'Don't wait up. Will you iron my Hawaiian shirt?'

Alexandra nodded, looking at him closely. 'Are you
all right? Your face looks a bit thin.'

He grinned and came to give her a peck on the cheek
as he left. 'I'm fine! Stop worrying.'

She couldn't help it. It was habit. She took the shirt
from the ironing basket and regarded it sourly, greatly
tempted to leave the iron standing on it. Of course he
was all right, and one of these days he would grow up.
What he would grow up into was the real problem.

Oddly enough, though, her mind didn't stay on Steven
at all—it went right back to Kyle Maddison. She was
anxious for no reason. She hadn't even met him yet.

When she saw the place that Eliot had chosen for dinner,
Alexandra felt very guilty. It was smart and expensive,
the sort of place she just could not afford, and she knew
that Eliot could not afford to come here either. He was
doing this to impress her and she merely felt friendly
towards him, nothing more. It made her very uneasy.

'Eliot,' she began carefully. 'You shouldn't have spent
so much just for a casual dinner.'

'I reckon you're worth it,' he assured her with a wide
grin, but that made things worse.

She looked at him worriedly. 'You know I'm just a
friend, Eliot.'

'I know. No harm in hoping though, is there?'

It wasn't a very good start to the evening, but she
tried. She was well dressed, at least. Her clothes were

carefully bought and carefully looked after, and she knew she looked smart enough for this place in her dark blue silky trouser-suit and high-heeled mules. She might have enjoyed it if Eliot hadn't been so smug about this, if he hadn't been so serious about her.

During the meal she began to have doubts about enjoyment. There was a feeling of being watched, and she soon got to the stage where she hardly dared raise her head. The feeling didn't last long, though. Annoyance set in and she looked up to stare round and see who was probing her mind.

It wasn't difficult to discover who, because the man watching her made no attempt at all to avoid her rather annoyed gaze. He simply went on staring at her with cold grey eyes until she blushed and looked hastily away.

She had the strangest feeling that she knew him. Certainly there was something familiar about him but his looks were far from friendly, and when she risked another glance at him he seemed to be coldly taking her apart. She didn't mention it to Eliot. He was like a dog with two tails, and if she brought up the subject of her embarrassment he would probably storm over and make a scene to impress her further.

She was glad when the meal was over but a little dismayed when Eliot wanted to dance. She would rather have left at once and even toyed with the idea of asking Eliot home for coffee, just to get out of there. She stifled the urge. It would give him even greater grounds for hope. She wasn't about to let a stranger force her into that.

At least the man couldn't stare at her when they were dancing, she thought with relief. His chair was sideways to the floor and he would have to be very deliberate to turn his head and watch.

He did better than that. He turned his chair, his cool grey eyes following every movement she made until she

could have walked over and shouted at him. She tried
a little staring herself. He looked tall, powerful and coldly
sure of himself, beautifully dressed, dark-haired. She had
just got to the stage of looking at his face when her nerve
gave out and she turned her head away quickly, glancing
appealingly at Eliot, who was holding her too close for
her liking.

'I'm a little tired, Eliot. Do you think we could go
now?'

'Of course,' he said quickly, not wanting to spoil
things. 'We've just about had our money's worth.'

As they left the floor, though, and Alexandra collected her bag, she heard Eliot's sharp indrawn breath
and glanced at him questioningly.

'We're being stared at with a certain amount of
dislike,' he said quietly, taking her arm and making for
the door. He glanced back and then hurried her out very
quickly indeed, his face a little flushed.

'We have as much right as anyone to be here,'
Alexandra said firmly, ignoring her own shaking knees.
'Just because that rude man is staring——'

'That man,' he muttered, ushering her through the
door with speed, 'is Kyle Maddison. If he looks like that
when he's having a good time, lord knows how he'll look
tomorrow when he comes in to chop us up.'

She remembered then where she'd seen the man
before—in the newspaper photograph. It didn't do him
justice. He looked much worse. Her heart sank to zero.

She was crossing the foyer next day and actually saw
him arrive. It was like seeing a foreign diplomat coming
to a meeting with no thought of compromise, and that
vague panic began to rise again inside her head.

He was flanked by two acolytes, both men, and they
came through the big doors almost line-abreast. She had
no difficulty in picking out Kyle Maddison. Even if she

hadn't seen him the night before, the power that seemed to surround him would have told her who this was.

He was tall and athletic-looking, beautifully dressed again, and he was probably the most ruthless-seeming man she had ever seen. Janey the receptionist darted out from behind her desk as it became clear that she was not about to be consulted, and Kyle Maddison stopped momentarily, looking down at her with a sort of cold surprise.

Alexandra's heart sank even further. Before last night she had cherished great hopes of him. Wasn't he the man to set things right? She wondered rather wildly just how tall he was. Of course, Janey was only small and it was probably his attitude that gave the impression that he was looking down from a great height.

He looked coldly unbending, quite above all this, quite above dealing with small firms like this too, but she knew why he had wanted this company. He had not long ago taken over a whole chain of hotels, and this neat little firm was sitting on very valuable land. There had been murmurs that he intended to extend the chain of hotels— certainly he was updating them. One had even been given a glowing write-up in the colour supplement of the Sunday paper that Alexandra took.

Raider! It seemed more likely, now that she'd seen him. Whatever plans he had for Fosdick-Kent, it would not be any sort of salvation. He would wind them up and walk out in the same cold, imperious manner.

She couldn't hear what he said but his words were few, his face unsmiling, and he strode across to the lift, his henchmen just one step to the rear as Janey darted back to her desk and the telephone. She was warning Gerald Norton. Kyle Maddison had known precisely where he was going.

Alexandra realised that she was still standing there, halfway across the foyer, and for a moment the same cool grey eyes lanced over her before he stepped into the lift. He turned, his eyes on her until the doors swished to, and she stared back as if she were hypnotised.

She was too stunned to move and her heart was hammering madly. It must be fear, because she had to admit that she felt something. Those startling grey eyes were utterly commanding, and soon she would have to face them close up. No doubt she would come to her senses and face him in the same way that she faced any trouble, but at the moment she was rather shakily impressed. The word 'dangerous' was ringing rather formidably in her head!

She looked up and caught Janey's eyes on her, and Janey made a very comprehensive sign. He was going to slaughter them all! Alexandra thought that too. Maybe Gerald Norton had not been far from the truth when he had said they were due to be stripped to the bone. It might very well be painful. It was a few minutes before she dared take the lift back up to her office. She had quite forgotten why she was down here in the first place.

Perhaps last night he had somehow known that she worked here—Eliot too. They might have reminded him about what he was going to do to this firm. She had few hopes of him now; in fact she had none at all, and she was annoyed to realise that she was very fluttery inside.

Nothing happened. She had expected instant action, people running hither and thither, but an unnatural quiet seemed to settle over the building and she buried herself neatly in her own office. Gerald Norton had at one time murmured the thought of her giving it up and moving into his office, but after her remarks about his interest in her he had let the matter drop.

She had always had this office. She had been the private secretary to the company as soon as Uncle Bob had considered that she had been efficient enough, and he had been a pretty hard taskmaster. She was more efficient than ever now, but she liked her little corner. Her office was snug and private.

How long would that privacy remain now? Soon Kyle Maddison would send for her—he could hardly do otherwise, as she had the affairs of the firm at her fingertips. She had all the personnel files too, and he would naturally want to see them. Who would he get rid of? Even if he kept the firm intact he would streamline the whole place, the offices and the plant. She sorted the files into age groups, going through them miserably. Some of the men had been here for years, almost since her Uncle Bob had started the firm. Would they be asked to take early retirement?

The end of the day came after what seemed like years, and she was glad that she hadn't to account for her time that day. It had been simply spent in waiting for a call that had never come. As far as Kyle Maddison was concerned, she didn't exist apparently. When it was time to go she shot off faster than she had ever done before.

The foreboding and anxiety were still there next day, and she hurried to her office with the distinct feeling that she was going to ground. She almost jumped out of her seat as the telephone rang.

'Miss Kent? I'm in the main office. Come across at once, please.'

She had never heard a voice quite like that before. It was deep and dark, quite beautiful, but oddly enough it alarmed her more than ever. If there was such a thing as an intelligent voice, this was it—coldly intelligent. She straightened her tan skirt and blouse, glanced at her appearance. Her hair was thick and straight. She never tried to curl it; having it well cut was the only trouble she went to. She smoothed her hands over it nervously and looped it behind her ears. This was it! She went across to his door, taking a deep breath and knocking softly before walking in. Her heart, she realised with a burst of astonishment, was beating like a hammer. It was perfectly ridiculous, because she didn't much care if he sacked her at once—she could get a job quite easily almost anywhere, so why was she feeling like this?

He was standing when she went in, his eyes already steadily on her as she turned from closing the door, and she thought that perhaps her heart knew what it was all about after all, because close up he really was alarming and at least six feet one or two. From the beautifully cut dark brown hair to the immaculate grey suit and the perfectly matching grey tie against a white shirt, he was the successful businessman.

He was much more than that, though. The cold, clear grey of his eyes proclaimed an intelligence in block capitals. He stood behind the big desk and regarded her steadily, a deep, assessing interest that was purely businesslike. There was no sexual appraisal—she was being summed up in a cool, intent way that made her feel like part of the office furniture.

'Sit down, Miss Kent.'

He motioned to the chair in front of his desk and she walked across to sit facing him, very conscious that he still stared at her in that intent, assessing way.

His cool eyes skimmed over her face, lingering on her soft mouth before moving to take in the neat but fashionable skirt and blouse. 'You're the private secretary for the company,' the cool, dark voice remarked. 'As the chairman was your uncle, I suppose that means you were his secretary.'

'Among other things. My uncle didn't believe in wasting time. All free minutes had to be occupied. I did the personnel work too.'

His long, carved lips twisted in the semblance of a smile that quite startled her. 'I can see why the company thrived. Did you have any other duties?'

'Not in any regular capacity.'

Actually, Uncle Bob had scraped every last minute of the day out of her, reminding her that she was family and not just some hired hand, although he had then proceeded to treat her like one.

'He had a certain reputation for toughness,' Kyle Maddison said wryly, and she knew he meant that Uncle Bob was reputed to be a skinflint. She couldn't argue with that!

'Since his death you have apparently been working with the general manager?' That gave him a few Brownie points—he hadn't said working *for* the general manager. She would rather have worked as a street sweeper.

'Yes.' She nodded quite pleasantly, telling herself that he was probably not too bad after all, but the smile died on her lips as he looked down at a file on his desk.

'I see from your file that you're——' he glanced down at the page '—insubordinate?'

'Only when provoked unduly!'

He was not going to give her much choice, so she took the bull by the horns.

'I take it that this was provocation of a personal nature?' His long finger tapped at her file.

'Not at all.' Now that it came right down to it, she didn't feel strongly enough to throw Gerald Norton to this particular wolf.

He looked up from beneath dark brows, his eyes steadily holding hers until she looked away, and she was quite certain he was well aware that she was lying.

So it was her turn first? She wondered if he had already seen some of the others. What had he made of Gerald Norton? No amount of blustering was going to get anyone past this man. How had he got her file without her knowing it? She didn't really have to ask that. Gerald Norton. Who else? Maybe she should have thrown him to the grey-eyed wolf after all.

She watched him as he read. He wasn't old, maybe thirty-five or six, certainly no more. The dark brown hair had no flecks of grey. It would be other people who went grey after meeting him! He was handsome in an uncompromising sort of way, but too hard-looking to be truly handsome. The fingers that turned her file were long and capable, his hands strongly graceful. Everything about him was expensive, from the wafer-thin gold watch to the beautifully tailored suit. Still, why not? He had made a fortune in these take-overs and there was a lot of slack in this firm, she knew that.

It had said in the paper that he was a multimillionaire, that his grandfather had been a wealthy Canadian businessman. Apparently he had more than quadrupled the money his family had left before he had been thirty. The Maddison Group was reputed to be deadly efficient. If he tightened things up here she couldn't really blame him. She had no doubt that he knew what he was doing, no matter why he had wanted Fosdick-Kent so badly.

The grey eyes glanced up and held her gaze and she felt her face flush. It wasn't at all nice to have a cold-faced, intelligent man looking over her file. The last man to handle that had been her Uncle Bob. She hastily corrected that—Gerald Norton had had it to pen in that little meanness about her insubordination.

He looked down again, one dark eyebrow raised at her expression. He almost made her shiver, but she watched him still with a sort of fascination. He was lightly tanned, his lips firm and long, his eyes thick-lashed. He looked so capable, rather frighteningly capable, and it wasn't any air of ruthlessness about him that had her heart uneasy. He didn't look at all cruel. There was just an air of inevitability about him. He got what he wanted. He expected to. Everything about him said so with confidence.

He was annoying her too! She wasn't really used to being held to account like this, and she had never before felt the rather odd anxiety she was beginning to feel all over again. Since she and Steven had lost their parents she had taken on a lot of responsibility, and she always had plenty at work here. She faced things squarely, but this man was making her think of ducking. It began to annoy her deeply.

CHAPTER TWO

'YOU'RE twenty-four.' Kyle Maddison's eyes were on Alexandra again as she looked up from her rather awe-stricken inspection of him, an awe-stricken inspection that was turning slowly to resentment. 'That seems to be rather young to have the responsibility that you've had. Personnel, too. It's difficult to imagine grown men bringing their problems to you.'

She could hear the quiet mockery and it added to her mounting annoyance. 'The problems are about work. I iron out difficulties—working difficulties. I don't run an agony column.'

She sounded a little too crisp and he pounced at once, a different line of attack. 'You have no business acumen, apparently. You sold half your shares when Fosdick-Kent shares were falling.'

'That's my private business! It has no reason to be in the file!'

'It isn't.' He looked up at her with mocking grey eyes. 'I happen to have been interested in the shares of Fosdick-Kent. I tracked all of them. Therefore I know you sold as they were falling.'

'You were making them fall, Mr Maddison! In any case, it made no difference. I didn't lose much.'

'You have financial problems, Miss Kent?' he asked drily.

'No! I do not! I'm quite comfortably off.'

'You have a younger brother.'

He seemed to know everything, but she hoped not. 'Yes.'

'He also has shares in the firm. Your uncle left you equal amounts. Not very many, considering you were the only family he had.'

'He also had a wife. Aunt Cora is still very much alive.'

'And a very stubborn lady,' he murmured grimly, the mockery dying and irritation taking its place. 'I sincerely hope that a thread of mulishness does not run through the family, Miss Kent?'

'She'll never sell her shares,' Alexandra said, an amused smile flickering across her lips. For once she felt in sympathy with Aunt Cora. To get the better of this man was really an achievement. 'She likes to speak out at the meetings.'

'She'll sell,' he muttered, his eyes intent on her face, obviously finding the smile quite out of place. 'I need a bigger grip on the firm and I have to have her shares. Therefore, your aunt will sell.' He looked away, his interest evidently gone. 'If you could bring the personnel files I'll start on them. Are they in any particular order?'

'Er—age,' Alexandra said uneasily.

'Oldest first?' He raised dark brows. 'You've lined up those easiest to get rid of?'

'As a matter of fact, the youngest are first.'

'Ah! You have no sympathy for your own generation.' His attitude of 'heads I win, tails you lose' brought a spark of further rebellion to her dark eyes. 'I prefer things to be in alphabetical order. Perhaps you could do that?'

'You've finished with me?' She could hardly keep the annoyance from her voice, and he regarded her steadily.

'Temporarily, Miss Kent.' He flicked a switch and spoke quietly. 'Come in here, Ian, will you?'

He was speaking to one of his shadows, Alexandra noted. She wondered where they were lurking.

'Give Miss Kent a hand with the personnel files, Ian,' Kyle Maddison ordered quietly as a young man came into the room. 'Alphabetical order. My secretary, Ian Jagger, Miss Kent,' he introduced briefly, adding sardonically, 'I prefer to have men around me at work.'

That left a lot of room for speculation about home. She found herself smiling at her own thoughts, her cheeks flushing as she looked up and found his eyes running over her. She could almost hear him cataloguing her appearance. Long fair hair, heavy and silky, dark eyes, with a soft sweetness at the back of a smattering of defiance, very slender.

His eyes stopped at her breasts, and she stiffened as an odd shiver ran over her skin. Resentment flared in her face and the cool grey eyes noted it unconcernedly—noted it with some astonishment, apparently. After all it had only been a brief inventory, and she even felt embarrassed that she had experienced that odd shiver.

Before the day ended, though, Alexandra was quite impressed. Twenty people had been interviewed and all had left looking happy, not one of them fired. Several had been more than ready to move to another firm that was under Kyle Maddison's wing. After the word had got around, at least four had actually asked to be moved, all of them with very good reasons, and Kyle Maddison had listened with patience and sympathy.

He had commandeered her services and she had sat taking notes, using each spare moment to watch him.

'You now have the general idea?' he asked quietly at the end of a tiring day. At least, it had been tiring for her—he looked as cool and controlled as he had done first thing. 'The aim is to build and not to destroy. During the process it is necessary to accommodate people—if possible. With no animosity we now have quite a few people willing to move—four even anxious to move.'

He leaned back in his chair and looked at her in a strangely patient manner, everything being considered, and she nodded, feeling a trifle humbled. He even managed a wintry smile.

'Good! Tomorrow I can safely hand the rest of the staff over to you. You will continue in like manner and report any difficulties to me. You will work in my office at the desk over there.'

'I have an office of my own,' she began quickly but got no further.

'I prefer you to work here,' he said crisply, offering no further explanation, and there was nothing she could do but nod obediently as she gathered up her things. 'Goodnight, Miss Kent.'

His voice was back to being derisive and immediately she was back to annoyance, her sneaking approval of him and her relief that she was not now available to work with Gerald Norton vanishing the moment he reverted to amused arrogance.

Over the next few weeks she never even saw Gerald Norton. How Kyle Maddison worked was no longer a mystery. He just never stopped, and everyone close to him was expected to keep up the same pace—especially her! She was there late night after night, even after Ian Jagger had gone, and it did not even lighten her feeling of resentment when her salary showed a remarkable increase for overtime. The fact that he too stayed and worked silently beside her, or, at least, in the same office, did nothing to excuse him. He simply asked her to stay late with no warning and no excuse.

She felt absolutely taken over, and it was not a good feeling. Each evening she felt as if she had to struggle to get away at all.

*   *   *

As she drove to work, Alexandra tried to hold down her private worries. She hadn't heard Steven come in last night and she didn't like the companions he had. He seemed to be slipping into the sort of life that would only end in trouble, more trouble than he had already. The boys he went around with thought that work was 'for the birds'—Steven had told her that more than once and she really felt that this time he wouldn't even try to get another job. He would have plans, though—he always had plans, and he worried her more each day.

Working in Kyle Maddison's office was also a strain, although he never bothered her and rarely spoke. She was aware of his presence, though, aware every minute of the time, and the knowledge made her rather sharp when she was obliged to speak to him. She resented the way he could draw her attention without doing anything at all, and she resented the way he coolly ordered her to do extra things when the day was over. Even Uncle Bob hadn't done that. Her assessment of what constituted a slave-driver was undergoing a change!

He had even called her up a home last night. He had seemed to have lost a file and it had nothing at all to do with her—it hadn't even been a file she had ever seen! He had expected her to know all about it, and had been grimly displeased when she had been a bit sharp. She had not been as sharp as she had felt. He thought he could keep her at work for all sorts of unsociable hours and then ring her at home.

She went into her own office, intending to stay there until he called her. He never seemed to make use of Ian Jagger. She had a feeling that he was taking it out on her because Aunt Cora wouldn't sell her shares. Since his arrival she hadn't been out in the evening more than three times, each time with Eliot Davis. Did the cool-eyed workaholic imagine she had no private life at all?

He called her before she had even removed her coat—
he must have some device hidden in her office to spy on
her! She marched along and went in with nothing more
than a very brief tap on the door, and as usual his eyes
were on her as soon as she appeared, looking no doubt
for that insubordination.

'You need me, Mr Maddison?'

Her dark eyes met his resentfully, and he looked back
with derision that was hardly veiled at all.

'Naturally. I rang.' He looked at her steadily for a
moment, his eyes running over her. 'Are you finding
things difficult, Miss Kent? You're looking a bit under
the weather, a trifle frayed at the edges.'

'I'm perfectly normal, thank you. Work and sleep are
supposed to be good for you.'

The dark eyebrows rose mockingly. 'Am I making you
miss the night-life, Miss Kent? I do apologise. Still, I
expect you realise that things are being pushed along
rapidly. It isn't going to last forever.'

'I don't mind at all, Mr Maddison,' Alexandra said
with a brittle smile. 'My uncle used to get work out of
people to the last drop of endurance. I'm quite used to
it.'

She expected anger but he confounded her as usual—
he laughed. 'I like hard work and loyalty. Get down to
all the files now and let me have a written report on your
conclusion before the end of the day.'

'I'll really try my best, Mr Maddison,' Alexandra
murmured starchily, giving him a chilly look before
walking to the desk he insisted she use and pulling the
great pile of files towards her.

If he thought he was going to keep this up he was
mistaken! There was nothing at all to stop her handing
in her resignation. Only the fact that Steven had now
decided to take up a life of leisure stopped her from doing
it right now. For two pins she would get up and——

'Your insubordination is showing, Miss Kent.'

The cool, deep voice made her jump, but apparently he was not infuriated; in fact, she was almost sure that she could hear him laughing. She didn't deign to reply.

It was a long day and she was determined to finish on time. She skipped lunch just to make sure. If he asked her to stay late tonight there would be a great big confrontation!

She pushed the last file back into the neat pile. Everything was finished, and after today she would not have to work here in this office. She flexed her shoulders and sighed deeply, her mind yet again on home and her problems.

'Tired?' The deep, dark voice made her jump. He had crossed the room and she hadn't even known. He was like a great big dangerous cat!

'Not really. I'm just a little stiff.' Alexandra knew that her voice was equally stiff, but he never seemed to notice. He noticed exactly what he wished to, and nothing more. 'I've finished,' she added hastily, standing and wishing she hadn't as the movement brought her dangerously close to the hard wall of his chest.

'I realise that. Tomorrow I'll lead you further into the workings of a take-over.'

'Oh! I'd expected to be in my own office from now on.'

'Doing what? Everything of importance takes place here at the moment, and your services are really valuable to me.'

'I really can't see how!' Alexandra managed a trifle crossly. To move she would have to brush past him, and he seemed to be utterly unaware of the trapped feeling she had standing here with her legs pressing against the desk to keep some sort of distance from him. 'Mr Jagger could do it, surely?'

'Call him Ian, do,' he murmured with a derisive look that told her she was altogether too young and childish. 'I wouldn't want him to get ideas above his station.'

His face was utterly cool, but she had the decided impression that he was laughing at her with a great deal of cruel relish. She often had that feeling now.

'Whatever!' she said curtly. 'You brought two assistants of your own and——'

'And lord knows what they do?' he finished for her sardonically. 'They assess, detail and report, Miss Kent. Carruthers is an accountant and Ian is a very private secretary. It's the private part that I like. In my line of business, one word out of place and shares go haywire.'

'I can imagine,' Alexandra managed with a small burst of sarcasm of her own. 'You wouldn't want them to see you coming.'

'Oh, they usually know when I'm coming, if I want them to. They certainly know when I've been. Right now, Ian is working on my next move.'

His voice was low and infinitely dangerous, and the same odd shiver as before ran down her spine and spread across her skin. It gave her goose-bumps, and she felt colour mounting under her skin. When you looked at things closely, he really was a dangerous man.

'Am I invading your space, Miss Kent?' He gave a slight smile that had the intent humour of a tiger about it. 'I apologise.'

He drew back and she hastily gathered her bag.

'I—I'll deal with these things in the morning,' she muttered, indicating the files. 'I'll get them back into their normal place.'

'Come straight in here as you arrive and we'll get to work at once,' he ordered. He still did not go back to his desk, but she had room to slip past him now.

'Yes, Mr Maddison.'

'Definitely insubordinate,' he informed her softly, adding quite unexpectedly, 'How close are you to Cora Kent?'

'Aunt Cora? I hardly ever see her.' She turned and looked at him in surprise. 'I try not to, anyway.'

'You don't get on well?'

'Reasonably well, but since our parents died she's taken an—an undue interest in us. She tries to interfere.'

'And you like to look after your brother all by yourself. I see.'

She faced him then, her gleaming head held high. What she did out of work was none of his affair, and right now she didn't seem to have any time out of work. 'You don't see, Mr Maddison! Stevie and I have been alone for over three years now. We have things exactly as we want them. We don't need any form of interference!'

'What does—Stevie do for a living?' The sarcasm of his voice was altogether too much, and right then he seemed to be prying into her life. Her own guilty conscience whispered that he knew about Steven's problems, and her lips tightened.

'He's a mechanic.'

'Really? Where does he work?' His probing made her more anxious than ever, and she did what she always did when under attack—she attacked back.

'He doesn't work here, Mr Maddison. That being the case, it's not really any business of yours!'

His voice was very reasonable, considering her tone. 'I take an interest in my staff and their families.'

'While ever the staff keep their jobs.'

This was ridiculous! He was probably being friendly, as close as a man like Kyle Maddison could be friendly, and here she was fighting every step of the way, throwing down the gauntlet to a cold-blooded man like this. He almost seemed to be making her do it!

'I wonder sometimes how long you'll keep your job, Miss Kent,' he said with a spark of hostility at the back of the clear grey eyes, although his face never changed.

'I don't much care.' She was tired and felt very harassed at this moment. He had moved closer again too, and that was worrying her.

'Which is most unfortunate, as I need you here quite badly. I'll have to work at it, won't I?'

'Anyone could fill my place,' she managed, fighting back a sudden panic.

'Not quite,' he murmured in that dark velvet voice. 'Perhaps you're tired. Goodnight, Miss Kent.'

Deep inside he must be furious, and she knew it. Why he was bothering to restrain his obvious inclination to fire her at once she had no idea. She turned swiftly to the door, feeling too tight inside to even say goodnight.

The feeling of dismay lingered even though she went out with Eliot, and the fact that Steven stayed out until three in the morning did nothing to help. She waited up, alternately dozing and worrying, and she was furious when he eventually dragged himself in. It was the usual excuse: a disco.

She had to be content with that and try to get some sleep. Tomorrow was Friday and she would be with Kyle Maddison all day, or, at least, she would be with him until he decided that she could retreat to her own little office. When this was all over he would be going. The time couldn't come soon enough for her!

Next morning he treated her as if nothing at all had happened. The night before she had almost talked herself out of a job, but he ignored it all. He glanced sharply at her tired face, but said nothing. She spent a few fruitless minutes trying to come up with some ideas of why she was of any value to a man like this, but she had to give it up as he began to work with his normal alarming drive, expecting exactly the same pace from her.

It was almost ten when his phone rang and she welcomed the break, leaning back to relax, until those cool eyes shot a strange look at her and he handed the phone across.

'For you, Miss Kent. A private call.'

It was very embarrassing, but her flushed cheeks turned pale as she heard Steven's voice at the other end of the line.

'Alex? I'm in trouble. I can make this call, but they're right here with me. They say you can come. Hurry up, Alex! They'll listen to you.'

Thoughts of kidnapping, of gangsters and other unlikely things flew through her mind. 'Where are you? Are you all right?' Her voice was sharp with anxiety and she forgot all about Kyle Maddison.

'The police station.'

'What? Stevie, what have you done?' It was like a blow to the heart, and she knew her hand was gripping the phone too tightly.

'I took a car. I went joy-riding.'

'Don't say anything,' she said urgently. 'If they're listening they'll write it all down! Don't get upset!'

'They don't have to write anything down, Alex! They caught me when I smashed the car up. For Pete's sake stop questioning me and come!'

Her hand was shaking so much that she could hardly write down the name of the place, and then she looked up at Kyle Maddison. 'I have to leave—right now.'

He nodded, his eyes curiously intent on her pale face. 'Feel free. Can I help?'

'No, thank you.' She just picked up her bag and ran.

She took a taxi with no thought of the cost because she felt utterly incapable of driving. Every dread she had anticipated was here, home to roost! The feeling of inadequacy choked her. How had she ever felt herself to be capable of taking care of Steven? His ways had been set long before she had given herself the task. He was a boy who felt himself to be a man, and only a man could have coped with him.

She knew perfectly well he deserved any punishment that would be given, but he was still too close to her heart, still her responsibility. No amount of logic could quell the feeling.

It was all sordid, embarrassing and frightening. By the time she arrived, Steven had slipped into another role she recognised only too well. The initial panic had gone and he was back to playing the big man, the charming rogue. Unfortunately the police had seen it all before and were not impressed. Any sympathy they had was for her.

'We've got him in court this afternoon, Miss Kent. There's so much petty crime now that we've a rapid method of dealing with it,' the sergeant said rather grimly. 'It's not much consolation to you, but at least he'll know his fate without a night in the cells. I can't offer any hope as to what the magistrate will say, though. They try not to put young people in prison, but he's done this before and he'll be facing a pretty tough lady.'

At the sight of her pale face the sergeant muttered angrily, and she was glad he didn't have the task of deciding punishment. His opinion of what Steven needed was written right across his face. He brought her a cup of tea, pointedly missing out Steven, who sprawled beside her with a very theatrical air of complacency that drew frowns from the rather fatherly sergeant with alarming regularity.

Alexandra had never been inside any sort of court before, and found it quite overwhelming. Steven's fate was right out of her hands and the knowledge terrified her. Chairing the court was a woman, and as the charges were read her eyes frequently went to Alexandra. It was almost possible to read her mind as she looked across then to Steven. He wasn't quite so complacent now, but even so there was an air of defiance about him that would do nothing to ease any sentence.

There was silence as the magistrates conferred over the file they had in front of them.

'I see that this young man has failed to report to his probation officer on several occasions.'

'Yes, madam.' A rather inadequate young man stood briefly and then sat down rapidly, getting himself a cold stare from the chairwoman.

A further conference ensued and then the stare was directed at Steven, who stood with some reluctance.

'This is the second time you have taken a car without the owner's consent.'

The third! Alexandra corrected silently, remembering her own badly smashed car.

'This time too you have crashed the car. You were driving without a licence, endangering the public and have caused a great deal of damage. Clearly you are not capable of self-discipline and have nobody capable of enforcing any discipline upon you. Before we can reach any sort of decision, perhaps we should hear from your sister?'

The rather outraged eyes were turned on Alexandra and she clasped her shaking hands together, unsure if she could speak at all. There wasn't a thing she could say in Steven's defence except point out that he had been ill for so long. She couldn't even say that. Her tongue seemed to be cleaving to the roof of her mouth.

'Madam Chairman, if you would give me permission to approach the Bench?'

The welcome interruption came from the back of the court and Alexandra turned grateful eyes in that direction, her gaze stunned as her eyes met the cool grey of other eyes. Kyle Maddison was sitting there and the man who had spoken was beside him—a lawyer, quite clearly, and an expensive one.

She just went on staring and quite deliberately he looked away, breaking the contact. She had the feeling that he was expecting her to speak or even shout, and his deliberate turning away was a warning. She was in fact quite incapable of speech or even of coherent thought. She had no idea why he was here, and his appearance hard on the heels of her distress about Steven left her quite lifeless.

It was hours since she had left his office. The thought reminded her that she had eaten nothing since breakfast, and that could perhaps account for the light-headed feeling she had. It could not account for it totally, though. She was beginning to get a light-headed feeling every time she saw Kyle Maddison!

They were called to the Bench—Alexandra, Kyle and a very intrigued Steven, who now looked more puzzled than brash.

'Astonishingly, Mr Maddison has undertaken to be responsible for you,' the chairwoman said severely. 'I hope you understand that this alone has saved you from detention? Quite clearly you are more than your sister can handle, and need a strong man around you. We are prepared to believe that Mr Maddison will exert the influence necessary. However, if you appear before us again I cannot think of anyone who would be able to save you. The conditions are that you live at Mr Maddison's house, report to your probation officer at the specified times and that all the damages shall be paid in full within one week from today.'

'I'll see to it that all that is carried out, Madam Chairman.'

The deep, dark voice cut through Alexandra's silent astonishment. She had been unable to utter a word. The tide of events had carried her onwards, and she now found herself deep into a situation that was unbelievable. She opened her mouth to protest, but Kyle's hand came like a grip of steel to her arm, quelling her words.

'As you will no doubt realise, Madam Chairman,' he said softly, 'Miss Kent is quite distressed by this. Such behaviour is utterly alien to her and to her family. I assure you that you will not be seeing the defendant again. I will take complete charge.'

Everyone seemed to be congratulating him, and Alexandra found herself ushered quickly outside, never having uttered a single word. It was beyond belief! She had to be dreaming. Steven was silent too, and the grim look on Kyle's face seemed to be the reason for that. Beside her, Steven seemed to be almost a man, no matter how she thought of him. Beside Kyle Maddison he was a mere boy, and he looked it.

'Into my car,' Kyle ordered after he had spoken quietly with his lawyer, and the mention of the word car brought Steven back to life with a snap.

'A Ferrari! Oh, boy!' He was instantly across to the bright red car, purring over it, his hand on the driver's door.

'In the back, Biggles!' Kyle's icy voice returned him to the present sharply. 'If you even breathe heavily on this car you'll be seeing things very hazily for days!'

The cold threat brought Alexandra out of her trance too, and her eyes were not too pleased as she saw Steven fold himself into the back of the car, his face downcast as Kyle unlocked the door.

'Look,' she said sharply, 'I think this needs some explanation.'

'Later!' He came round and helped her in with a smooth disregard for her opinions. 'We'll call work over for today. I'm taking you both with me, and when we get home we'll have any discussion you like. Meanwhile, try to keep silent. I'm not normally given to playing Fairy Godmother and the temper is a little ragged at the moment.'

She could see that and, after all, he had just rescued Steven—rescued them both! Why he had done it she did not know, and how they were going to get him out of the promise to have Steven living at his home was something of a puzzle. Obviously he hadn't meant it, but he had probably already worked out his strategy with that very smart-looking lawyer. She could only wait and see.

Steven was quite silent and she glanced at him anxiously, only to find that he was utterly given up to watching the performance of the car, his narrow escape from confinement behind bars dismissed from his mind. It was madness! He probably needed psychiatric help. Kyle looked more inclined to offer violence. His cold face was without expression, and she swallowed nervously as her eyes left their contemplation of his strong, graceful hands. He was handling the car so beautifully that Steven must be impressed. He was—he never said a word.

They were miles outside London before Kyle turned off the motorway, and he had not spoken once. None of them had, but Alexandra had done a lot of thinking. She found herself in an incredible situation. This man, who sat so silently beside her in a speeding car, was nothing more than a stranger. Out of the blue he had stepped forward, rescued her brother, suffered the embarrassment of appearing at a magistrates' court and taken charge. He didn't look embarrassed, she had to admit that. She glanced at him out of her eye-corner, then looked away again rapidly, overwhelmed by his sheer, cold, hard masculinity.

The expression 'out of the frying-pan, into the fire' came into her head, and her small, even teeth bit down on her lip. One thing was sure: she would have to watch her step at work in the future. Her days of standing up to him seemed to be over. Both she and Steven owed him too big a debt of gratitude, but why he had done it was uppermost in her mind.

The car turned into the long drive and she realised that they had arrived. It was a country estate, and quite big by the look of the drive, which seemed to go on for a very long time. Wooded parkland stretched at either side and, as she gazed around, the house came into view.

It was big, Georgian and very imposing. For the whole of her life, Alexandra had been used to living in a modest house. Even the large house that her uncle had bought when Fosdick-Kent Plastics had really taken off had been modest compared with this, and if she hadn't known it before she would have been in no doubt now that Kyle Maddison was a very rich man.

The Ferrari growled to a halt at the front of the house, and Kyle took a deep breath that seemed to be a further attempt to control anger. 'Welcome to Downham Manor. Home.'

There was something about his tone that brought Alexandra's eyes round to his face with one swift movement, and he turned slowly, meeting her gaze, the clear grey eyes deeply assessing.

'We find ourselves in an unusual situation, Miss Kent,' he said curtly. 'Before we look further into it, I imagine a snack of some sort would be advisable. You probably haven't eaten for hours.'

He got out then and came round to help her. She noticed that he didn't wonder whether or not Steven had eaten. He would probably like to lock him in an attic and let him starve. The sooner she got away from here, Steven with her, the better. Kyle Maddison would have some plan worked out. She could safely leave it to him.

CHAPTER THREE

THE inside of the house lived up to all that the outside had promised. Stevie seemed to be dumbfounded and Alexandra felt pretty much the same. It was almost palatial. There seemed to be acres of shining floor in the huge circular hall, and as they entered a white-haired man came from one of the rooms.

'Oh, Mr Maddison! Miss Hepwarth called. She tried to get you at the office but apparently you'd gone out.'

'Thank you, Graves. I'll ring her later. Could you bring us a few sandwiches and some coffee? We missed lunch. We'll have them in the drawing-room.'

'Certainly, sir.' The man gave Steven a curious look and then smiled pleasantly at Alexandra. 'I'll just take your coat, miss.'

She felt like clinging on to it and maintaining a stance at the front door, but reason won and she managed a smile of her own.

'A butler, yet!' Steven's whisper was not lost on Kyle as Graves departed in a dignified manner.

'As your sister will tell you, I prefer to have men around me,' he said curtly. Steven preened, but Alexandra could have told him that the pleasant thought did not include a seventeen-year-old with a penchant for wrecking cars. No doubt he was about to find all that out for himself.

Kyle, however, said nothing. The sandwiches were served and they all ate in silence, a state of affairs that never seemed to bother Kyle Maddison—she had noticed that at the office. Her own tension mounted higher

40

and higher, though, and after a while he looked across at her and then felt in his pocket.

'I have to talk to your sister,' he said directly to Steven. 'Meanwhile, there's something I want you to do.' He held up a bunch of keys and selected one. 'Behind the house are two garages. This key is for the second one, the largest. Go in there and look around. You can tell me what you think when you get back here—take your time.'

Steven's face was a mixture of puzzlement and rapture. The word garage spelt cars and he was off with some alacrity, but Alexandra looked at Kyle as if he were quite mad.

'Now the grown-ups can talk,' he said sardonically, looking at her as if she were merely a child herself and quite likely to misbehave.

'A garage? Cars?' she asked with a shocked look.

'None ready for the road,' he assured her, but she shook her head.

'You don't know Stevie. He's a mechanical genius.'

'Among other things,' he said grimly, adding, 'I know. I had a long talk with his probation officer while you were sitting waiting for his case to come up.'

'Why have you done this?' she asked urgently. 'How did you know? How did you——?'

'To take things in chronological order,' he began, 'I heard your call. I knew you had trouble. I came out at once to give you a lift but you were already in a taxi. I followed, but when I saw your destination I very much doubted whether you would welcome a stranger at that time. However, I did find out a few pertinent facts from the sergeant and I contacted my lawyer. The rest you know.'

'I don't, though.' Her eyes sought to hold his and not look away. It took some courage but she managed it. 'I know how you did it, but not why. You're a stranger, as you just admitted.'

'Not for long, I think.' He managed to make that sound very grim indeed. 'You are called Kent. The Boy Wonder is called Kent. My reasons are quite simple: I do not want any adverse publicity at this time when I'm still trying to get more control of the company. It's surprising how the newshounds track me. Secondly, you have an Aunt Cora who is going to sell her shares to me. She doesn't realise that fact yet, but she will.'

'I don't see what that's got to do with——'

'Don't you, Miss Kent?' he enquired derisively. 'I hold a pretty big sword over your head. If I break my word, tell that rather frosty lady on the Bench that your brother is more than sanity can bear, then I really think that this time he'll be behind bars. Ladies like that don't take kindly to youths who go joy-riding in stolen cars. Ladies like that have cars of their own and they think about such things.'

'He didn't steal——' Alexandra began heatedly, but he stopped that line of argument at once.

'Taking without the owner's consent is not stealing? What then is it?'

'He never meant to steal,' she muttered, her eyes at last falling before the blaze of clear grey.

'Perhaps next time he'll have criminal contacts, after he's been in prison,' Kyle said in a hard voice. 'There's always a good opening for someone with mechanical ability. Next time he'll probably be told what make and year to steal.'

'He's not going to prison!'

Her frantic voice seemed to please him, because the hard rasp left his tone.

'Then we must plan the present and hope mightily that the future is retrievable.' He looked at her steadily. 'While you're both living here you can leave him to me for most of the time. I'll plan his future and see that he toes the line.'

Alexandra looked at him in silence for a second or two. The shivers were back again, running down her spine. 'I—I don't think I've really been listening,' she began. 'You intend to keep Stevie here?'

'I gave my word to the lady on the Bench. His release is solely because of that. Where I live and how I live was carefully explained to her by my lawyer. It impressed her. He's a long way from town.'

'He'll—he'll be a nuisance.'

'We'll handle him.'

It brought her to the most worrying thing about this. 'I'm not living here!' She was rather proud of the firm voice, but he was not too impressed.

'You think I'm taking on Attila the Hun alone? He needs us both. I need us both! You stay here, Miss Kent, or the lady on the Bench gets a polite note of regret.'

'It was all your idea,' she snapped, feeling herself drown in unreality. 'You're the big man who can manage anything. The lady on the Bench seemed to be pretty sure of that. There was no mention of me except as a rather inadequate parental substitute!'

'Don't take it to heart, Miss Kent,' he advised wryly. 'You're little more than a girl yourself. I have the years and the necessary weight. You can simply see that fair play is done and you can baby-sit when I go out.'

'I'm not staying here!' She stood angrily, stung by the derision in his voice, and he stood too, coming to tower over her.

'Then he goes back to court,' he assured her softly. 'You weren't actually included in the original package, but I decided to include you. What can you lose? This is a big house, we can dodge around each other easily and I'll take you to work each day with no trouble.'

'And who baby-sits then?' she asked sharply.

'Ah! Wait until he comes back. I'm quite cunning. Clever beyond my years.'

The grey eyes were laughing, and to her consternation a vibrant feeling of recognition swept over her. She stepped back, rejecting it with all speed. Her skin was hot, something inside her quivering. She looked away quickly, trying to recover. 'You—you know that all this is quite ridiculous.'

'Funnily enough, I had expected some small gratitude,' he mused. 'Nothing elaborate, you understand? Just little things like "thank you" and "whatever you say". Belligerence I did not anticipate, but then again you *are* insubordinate. I already know that. You look quite gentle too. How odd. There again, your brother looks a real lamb at heart. You never can tell.'

This bantering, the look in his eyes, made her nervous and she sat down with a rush. 'I—I'll give it a try.'

'Good! Six months' probation, that was the lady's last word as I recall. We'd better get you both settled in here.'

'Six months! I can't stay here for six months!'

'Ah! Eliot Davis just won't like it?' he queried sharply, and she grasped the straw with both hands even though she was stunned that he knew anything about her private life.

'Quite true,' she lied. 'He'll not like it at all.'

'He can visit you here and you can go out from here. Of course, he can't sleep with you here, not under my roof.'

'I do not sleep with Eliot!' she said hotly, hastily giving Eliot more room in her life than a few dinner dates allowed. She was only complicating things further, and he was taking a devilish delight in allowing her to do just that.

'So, what other problems do we have?' He looked at her flushed face and sat down again, taking out a black cheroot and lighting it.

'Oh, none. I'll stay!'

'I thought you would,' he assured her quietly. He was utterly ruthless! She had been wrong about him before. She stared at him, her soft dark eyes angry, and he looked straight back with no expression at all.

'Is there anything else before Stevie comes back?' she snapped finally when it became apparent that he was not about to say anything at all.

'A few things, the name being one of them. We are about to impress upon your brother that he is an adult with responsibilities. It would perhaps be advisable to allow him to have an adult name.'

'He's always been called Stevie.'

'And look where it got him. In future he will be Steven.' Apparently the matter was at an end, and she nodded.

'Next, the matter of the payment of damages and the rather substantial fine. The total, if you remember, comes to five thousand pounds. He doesn't take cheap cars.'

'I'll—I'll have to get the money——' she began in a more subdued voice, embarrassed again, but his voice cut across hers, unusually crisp.

'Steven will pay. He did the damage. He must learn that things have consequences.'

'But he doesn't have any money. I can sell my shares.'

'Now we come to it. You did that before didn't you, the last time he went joy-riding? No! He can sell his shares. He can sell to me and he can pay the money like the man he thinks he is.'

'That's all there is to this, isn't it?' she snapped. 'You want our shares.'

'Have I told you yet that you're an ungrateful little wretch?' he asked quietly. 'I'm not in the business of collecting minutiae. I want Cora Kent's shares. I have fifty-five per cent of the shares now and she has thirty per cent. When I have those, the rest I will gobble up.'

'And us with them,' she suggested angrily.

'When you feel like being devoured,' he murmured drily, 'just let me know, Miss Kent.'

They were no longer talking about shares, she was sure, and her face flushed slowly as his eyes began an inspection of her that was no longer businesslike. She knew he was merely punishing her in a very masculine way, but she couldn't stop the shudder that raced through her with almost frightening pleasure. Since he had come to the firm he had managed to get under her skin, to make her feel aware of him by doing absolutely nothing at all. Now, with those grey eyes on her so speculatively, it was suddenly difficult to even breathe.

The grey eyes suddenly narrowed and she saw for the first time a smile, long and slow, a very male recognition. 'Well, well,' he murmured softly.

Fortunately the telephone rang and he reached out for it, his eyes still lazily appraising her. 'Oh, Dulcie! How are you, sweetheart? No, not tonight. I have a whole evening of work ahead of me. I'll contact you in the morning, but don't bank on tomorrow even. At the moment I have two really big responsibilities.'

Alexandra flushed and looked away as he watched her derisively, and after listening for a moment he said goodbye and put the phone down.

'I can see that we're going to interrupt the smooth flow of your life,' Alexandra said tartly, her tongue running away with her.

'Not really,' he said simply. 'I adapt to changing circumstances.'

'I wonder if Graves will?' she snapped.

'He'll see things my way, I'm sure. Everyone does— eventually.'

He seemed to be trying to frighten her, but the only thing that frightened her was the vibrant force that reached out across the intervening space and actually seemed to surround her.

'I can't stay here,' she managed in a choked voice, and once again she was at the receiving end of that unusual smile that seemed to change his whole personality.

'Of course you can, Alexandra,' he assured her softly. 'You can stay here and for once you can relax. You'll know exactly where that brother of yours is both day and night. I have plans for him.'

'I had plans for him,' Alexandra said bitterly, shocked that she felt comforted because he had called her by her first name. 'He ignores them.'

'He won't ignore my plans, I can assure you.'

If he did there would be more trouble than Stevie—Steven—could handle. Kyle's quiet voice said that clearly.

'What—what are you going to do? He's not strong. He's been ill for years.' The grey eyes narrowed on her pale face, his expression intent.

'Is that how we've reached this sorry state of affairs? I thought it was only old ladies who played on past ill health.'

'He doesn't play on it!'

'But you remember it and he lets you? I think you both need rescuing, Alexandra. While you're here you'll perhaps discover that you have rights and needs too.'

She suddenly wanted to cry and she didn't know if it was with relief or anxiety. It seemed as if without warning everything in her life had steadied and become secure. She gave him a bewildered look and that smile flashed out again and seemed to surround her.

'Maybe when I've dealt with Steven I'll have time to deal with you,' he murmured, his amusement growing at the sight of her flushed face.

When Steven came in he looked at Kyle with some awe.

'There's a Bugatti in there!' He turned to Alexandra with really boyish eagerness. 'Alex! He's got a garage full of vintage cars. It's like a treasure-house!'

'There are four, to be exact.' Kyle's eyes were now intent on Steven. 'I've been collecting them for some time.'

'Do you drive them?' There was a strange kind of rapport between the cool man and the eager boy, and Alexandra was almost holding her breath.

'In the grounds sometimes. I don't get much chance. Only one is in running order at the moment in any case. I only just acquired the Bugatti.'

'It needs a lot of work on it. I had the bonnet up. The parts will have to be made, but I know a man down by the docks who could make everything you need.' Steven's voice quickened to eagerness and Kyle nodded with a great deal of satisfaction.

'I hoped you'd say that. Tomorrow you can make up a list of what's needed and when it's finished we'll talk it over and get along to see this friend of yours. Think you could work on the Bugatti by yourself?'

'Could I?' Steven's enthusiasm was almost tangible, then his face fell. 'It's worth a small fortune, Mr Maddison.' He looked worried but Kyle smiled.

'Your sister tells me you're a mechanical genius. I'm prepared to take a chance if you are—and call me Kyle.'

'I'll have it good as new. Better!'

'You need a haircut,' Kyle suddenly said crisply, and Alexandra looked anxiously at her brother. The words were familiar—she had said them herself several times and got a sharp reply.

'OK. I'll get it trimmed tomorrow.' Steven looked less than pleased now. 'I'll drop in to the shop and——'

'You'll go to my hairdresser,' Kyle corrected. 'It will be cut, not trimmed. I do not need a yellow-haired parakeet hanging around my house!'

'I'd never get through the door of your hairdresser,' Steven said sullenly. 'People like that don't take people like me.'

'They do if they want to keep people like me,' Kyle assured him shortly. 'I'll go with you.'

It was the end of the matter. Steven knew better than to argue and that was clear. Alexandra felt really superfluous and as Steven went to wash his hands, now well covered with grease, Kyle turned to her with a wry smile.

'You see? It's easy.'

'If you've got the Golden Touch.'

'And I have?'

'So they say. You don't need me here at all. Quite obviously he'll obey any order to get at the cars, and equally obviously he's not going to leave that garage ever unless he needs spare parts.'

'I do need you here, Alexandra. Things have begun well but I doubt very much if they'll continue so smoothly. It's like offering a child a toffee bar. Things are quiet—until he's eaten it.'

'Why, then you'll just buy another Bugatti!' There was a touch of bitterness that she even recognised herself, and Kyle stood and walked towards her.

'They're not so easy to come by,' he said softly. 'I don't intend to go on offering the toffee either. Discipline comes from within.'

Another thing she had said often—remarks on to deaf ears.

'He may wreck the Bugatti. What then?'

'But I have faith in your word,' he assured her ironically. 'You promised me a mechanical genius.' He suddenly laughed, that low, amused sound that sent ripples of unexpected feeling right through her. 'Don't worry, I have enough mechanical knowledge myself to know if he's any good. As he said, the Bugatti is worth a small fortune, and I don't let things slip through my fingers. I get what I want.'

Funnily enough those words alarmed her, and he watched her intently for a few minutes well aware of her feelings and then, as Steven walked back into the room, Kyle moved away and said briskly, 'Right. We'll need to drop over to your house to collect a few things for this evening. Tomorrow we'll get the rest of your clothes and personal effects.'

'What about——?' Steven began, his eyes on Alexandra, but Kyle spoke before she could.

'Your sister is moving in here, too.'

'He's asked you to live with him?'

Alexandra blushed hotly—she didn't like Steven's grin, and neither did Kyle apparently. One long brown finger jabbed the air in the direction of Steven's face.

'If you're pretending to be a man, remember that manners are a necessary commodity. You can't survive without them here. Sly innuendo is something I can well do without!'

His instant black anger obviously scared Steven. It was years since anyone had spoken to him like that. 'I—I'm sorry, Mr Maddison.' He really looked sorry too, Alexandra mused in a small daze.

'Kyle. As to apologising to me, I don't particularly feel slighted. Alexandra was the one you insulted. It's a privilege to have her under my roof. I doubt if she'll allow it to be a pleasure.'

'I'm sorry, Alex.' He didn't seem to have got the gist of Kyle's remarks and Alexandra wasn't sure what was making her face more red—the remarks or the really genuine apology. She had the feeling that they would both leave this house changed characters.

Graves took it all in his stride and announced that rooms would be ready by the time they returned. Kyle too seemed to think nothing of the journey back to

London. There was a feeling of things being pre-ordained, and Alexandra found it difficult to speak at all.

They were settled smoothly into the rather grand household and Steven had an early night without so much as a murmur. Throughout dinner he had talked solidly about the Bugatti, his confidence with Kyle growing very quickly, and Kyle had seemed quite content to confine his conversation to that and to Steven. Alexandra had had nothing to say at all, but her eyes had gone surreptitiously to the cool, clever face whenever she'd thought he hadn't been looking.

She was as much in awe of him as Steven was. It was all so incredible. Such a short time ago she had not even set eyes on this man and now she was here, unwillingly it was true, but here nevertheless. Her brother was firmly under his wing and their lives were to be ordered smoothly. The office seemed miles away, totally unreal.

On Saturday morning he produced an Audi Estate. Obviously they could not get all their things into the Ferrari, and the fact that he seemed to have a chain of expensive vehicles at his disposal impressed Steven further. Alexandra had just come to expect it—or anything else for that matter.

At their house they were confronted by Mrs Nash, and Alexandra felt a quick burst of embarrassment as she wondered what to say, knowing that questions would be forthcoming.

'You're the very good neighbour? I've heard so much about you,' Kyle lied cheerfully, surreptitiously urging his charges inside. He actually stood there talking to her and Steven grinned once they were safely indoors.

'Wonder what he'll tell her?' he asked, clearly not at all worried if everyone knew about his problems.

'He'll talk as long as he thinks it necessary and tell her precisely nothing,' Alexandra snapped. 'You don't know Kyle at all, Steven. Watch your step.'

'Steven,' he grumbled. 'He's got you under his thumb.'

'And you!' Alexandra rounded on him sharply. 'If you think he'll let you do one thing that he disapproves of then you can think twice or even more than that!'

Her nerves were on edge and she realised it. She bit her lip and turned away. She wasn't used to quarrelling with Steven and it was all because she felt so uneasy about this unexpected turn of events. She had nothing at all to do with this, she reasoned. Kyle had taken it upon himself to alter Steven, but she was now trapped too. The unfairness was bubbling just below the surface and she was taking it out on her brother instead of Kyle Maddison.

He came in then and caught the expression on her face, and his own expression hardened. 'We'll get along to the hairdresser's and see if he can cope with you,' he said to Steven. 'Leave your packing until later, or maybe Alexandra could do it for you while we're out?'

'Why not?' she muttered, half to herself. 'After all, I'm merely an irritated onlooker in these astonishing events.'

'We'll get you something else to wear too, Steven,' Kyle said tersely, his eyes narrowed and cold on Alexandra.

'I've got clothes. I like what I wear!' Defiance edged Steven's voice and Alexandra shot a quizzical look at Kyle, which only annoyed him further.

'I don't!' He tossed Steven the keys. 'Wait for me in the car.'

Steven's face was sullen again and as the door closed behind him Alexandra turned away, but Kyle pounced on her at once.

'Your resentment is written all over your face,' he bit out and her temper flared at once as she swung to face him.

'And why not? You're Steven's saviour, not mine. I don't know what this is all about but I suspect there's more to it than gentle charity and the desire to avert bad publicity.'

'And you know that I'm neither gentle nor charitable, of course?' His face was back to cold aloofness and it irritated her further.

'You're a man I work for, temporarily. I don't know you from Adam!'

One strong hand shot out and slid under her hair, closing round the back of her neck, the grip tightening as he pulled her inexorably closer.

'Let me go!' she flared at him, her dark eyes flashing with anger, but he ignored any order, pulling her closer until the grey eyes seemed to fill her vision with nothing else left.

'You don't know me from Adam,' he lashed out coldly. 'I'm about to introduce myself!'

His arm came round her waist and their bodies touched. It was a shock she had not expected, an indescribable feeling, and she reacted violently, fright flooding through her. Her hands pushed at the hard wall of his chest as she struggled frantically, some instinct warning her to keep him at a distance on a permanent basis. 'Stop it, damn you!'

He merely tightened her to him, his hand on her neck like a vice as he bent to crush her lips with his own. She struggled, but only momentarily. The cruelty was short-lived. His fingers speared into her hair and the strong hand cradled her head as he gathered her close, and the kiss changed.

It shattered her. It was timeless, brief but unending. For seconds she lost all sense of reality as a curtain of stars seemed to come down and enclose them both. It was soothing, possessive and searing all at the same time, robbing her of any will, and when he lifted his head she stared at him with dazed eyes.

It seemed to be a long time before she could speak, and all the time the grey eyes watched her, his face expressionless.

'You—you had no right to do that,' she whispered, too stunned even now to move from his grasp. 'It was...'

'Wicked? Insensitive? Unforgivable?' he enquired helpfully, disdain on his cool face. 'For a few seconds, Alexandra, you were mindless.'

'It was shock!' She pulled away abruptly and he let her go, still with that sardonic look about him that assured her he knew perfectly well what had happened to her. The aloof arrogance gave her a quick rush of courage.

'Ever since you came to the firm you've been there every time I've turned around, and now you've insinuated yourself into my private life! I don't like you, Mr Maddison, and I don't trust you one inch. I'm not surprised that people are scared of you. It's easy to be ruthless when you have no normal standards of behaviour!'

'Coming from someone whose brother breaks the law with impunity, that's certainly rich. What I *have* done is rescue your brother from a sentence in prison.' The anger was back in his voice and she decided she felt safer like that. 'The only reason you're living in my house is that I flatly refuse to take the responsibility on single-handed. I have a life of my own.'

'So do I!' she said wildly.

'Then he'll just have to wait,' Kyle snapped. 'Get on the phone and explain it to him while we're out. Tell him you're going to live with your boss!'

'I'm not!'

'It looks suspiciously like it, though, doesn't it?' The tigerish humour was back again as he turned to the door. 'Refuse, and you know exactly what I'll do.'

'I don't think you would,' Alexandra murmured, looking at him with a rather lofty defiance.

'May I remind you, Miss Kent that you don't know me from Adam?' he pointed out coldly.

'Why are you doing all this? Why did you rescue Steven in the first place?' Her dark eyes held his as she tried once again to see into the depths of his mind, to sort out this great puzzle that had left her trapped and utterly defenceless.

He looked at her steadily, a slow smile growing on the hard planes of his face. 'I always try to be one jump ahead of everyone. With you it's not at all difficult.' He moved to the door. 'We'll be about two to three hours. When we get back I'd like to leave fairly quickly, so see what you can do.'

'I—I'm sorry,' she offered shakily, suddenly realising that he was after all almost a gaoler as far as Steven was concerned. Keeping on the right side of him would perhaps be a better idea than taking up any fighting stance.

'You're not,' he said scathingly. 'What you are is scared. It's interesting that you fight instead of crying. But then I suppose your desire to defend that odd youth who is probably even now toying with the idea of taking my car is always uppermost in your mind. Quite the little mother, aren't you?' He suddenly looked more grim than ever. 'Believe me, Miss Kent, I have no designs on your virtue. Just try to behave a little better than Steven does and you'll be quite comfortable and perfectly safe.'

The safety factor was not really in his control, she mused as he left and banged the door shut. That kiss had left her almost stunned. She would be a lot safer if he kept his distance. Not even then, she corrected. The feeling of recognition had been there almost from the first. She began to pack with a certain vicious energy, wondering exactly what she had been drawn into, Gerald Norton's dire words racing around in her head. One thing was sure—he wasn't going to strip any assets from her!

By Monday morning Alexandra had to admit that she was no longer in control of anything. She tried her best to keep quiet because another outburst would probably bring the same kind of punishment and she wasn't at all sure how she would survive it, or even if she would at all. Kyle's grey eyes were subtly different, glinting with a new knowledge. He too remembered the way she had reacted to him and it was not a comfortable feeling. He had a weapon for chastising her, and she dared not bank on his keeping Steven out of prison if she just walked out.

During Sunday she had overheard another telephone conversation between Kyle and the still unseen Dulcie Hepworth, and it had embarrassed her badly. The phone had rung while she had been in the drawing-room and she had made to leave, but he had motioned her back to her seat, clearly not caring what she heard.

'Of course I want to see you, darling. I've been too busy this weekend but I'll come over to your flat on Monday evening. Of course I do. I'm desperate.'

His voice had lowered seductively and Alexandra had jumped up to leave. He had certainly sounded desperate! If he'd needed the company of his lady-love so much why had he been wasting his time with Steven and her? The only good reason had seemed to be Aunt Cora, though why he thought she would be kindly inclined at his rescuing Steven, Alexandra had had no idea. Cora Kent would not have hesitated to let Steven face the consequences of his actions. She had disapproved of his up-bringing right from the first and had regarded his illness with suspicious eyes.

Kyle Maddison was being denied the pleasure of Dulcie's arms for nothing. And it had suddenly dawned on her who Dulcie Hepwarth was anyway. The Miss Hepwarth had not run any particular bell, but Dulcie Hepwarth had been different. Eliot had only recently been complaining he couldn't get tickets for *Under the Rainbow*, the musical hit that everyone was trying to see. Dulcie Hepwarth was the star, her singing and dancing the talk of the theatre world.

He must have been determined to get at Aunt Cora if he had been prepared to forgo Dulcie Hepwarth's company for even one night, she was so beautiful and talented. Aunt Cora would never sell her shares, so he was wasting his time, giving up his lady-love for nothing. Aunt Cora liked playing the grand lady and she thoroughly enjoyed the sound of her own voice.

'Where are you off to?' His cool, deep voice had hit her as she'd made for the door.

'To my room. I don't really like listening in to other people's telephone calls.'

Her face had been flushed and she'd turned to glare at him, admitting to herself that it had been a mistake as soon as she'd seen his face.

'Don't you? If you were on the phone I'd really love to listen.'

'But then, you're different, aren't you?' she'd snapped, her face flushed. 'You must have done a lot of spying to get where you are.'

He had only been amused at her anger. 'Where am I, after all?' he'd mused softly. 'You look just like a jealous wife, Alexandra.'

She had stormed out of the room, her hands clenched by her sides. Just what was he up to? She didn't trust him one inch!

Alexandra heard Cora Kent's voice much sooner than she had anticipated. Kyle drove her to work, having given Steven his orders for the day, and Alexandra had to admit that for once she felt quite happy about leaving Steven to his own devices. He had been impatient to get round to the garage and she knew that he was happily settled for some time to come. He looked better too. The haircut was really beautiful and so were the expensive and simple jeans and sweatshirt. A good night's sleep hadn't done him any harm either. He might get back to really good health here.

If she could just have left him to Kyle and gone about her own business everything would have been fine. He wasn't about to let her do that, though. He had ordered Steven to bed the night before and then had told her curtly that she seemed very tired. The fact that he had been quite right had done nothing to make her feel pleased. They were going to be well-fed prisoners! It was his fault that she had been tired too. He had worked her to death since he had been at the firm. He had even seemed reluctant to let her off the hook when it had been late and pitch-black outside. She had sat silently by him all the way to work, and he was utterly indifferent to her, too.

CHAPTER FOUR

KYLE called a meeting of the office staff on Tuesday and told them coolly exactly what was happening. It seemed that a collective sigh of relief ran round the room and they all trooped out happily, except Gerald Norton. He hung back to impress on the others that his position was more important. Alexandra was walking out with Eliot and Janey when Kyle's voice stopped her.

'Stay here, Alexandra. I need you for a few hours.'

Her face flared with colour at his tone. It was quietly possessive, astonishing her, and both Eliot and Janey shot her looks of surprise. Everyone knew she had been working up here, *and* grumbling about it, night after late night, but his voice was darkly caressing, giving another aspect to it entirely. They had no idea that she was one of two prisoners he held. Nobody had seen her arrive with him and she intended to take her own car back tonight so that nobody would in future.

She avoided looking at Gerald Norton, and her heart fell right to her boots as she heard Cora Kent's loud and insistent voice in the outer office.

'My dear young man, I am Cora Kent! Of course Mr Maddison will see me now. I insist upon going right in!'

She just walked in, an outraged Ian Jagger behind her, and Kyle smiled wryly at him.

'Of course I'll see Mrs Kent immediately, Ian,' he said smoothly. 'Just close the door, it's quite all right.'

The sight of Alexandra stopped Cora's voice, however, and she marched across as if nobody else were in the office. 'Alexandra! I rang you all day yesterday and even late at night. Nobody answered. Where were you and that wretch of a Steven? I hope you were together. I do not approve of either of you being out as late as eleven, and if he's still pretending to be ill, *that's* not going to get him better!'

Alexandra was dumbfounded. Cora certainly had the bit between her teeth. It was interfering day! She suddenly realised that she hadn't the faintest shadow of an excuse ready. She was still reeling from Kyle's tone and she was quite sure that if she told her aunt to mind her own business he would be furious. He took matters out of her hands.

'I'm sorry if you were worried, Mrs Kent,' he murmured, handing her a card. 'Here's my home number. If you want Alex again just ring here. She's living with me, and of course Steven has moved in too. It's a big house.'

There was utter silence. Kyle moved round to place a chair in front of the desk for Cora Kent but she stood like stone, her mouth partly open as Alexandra's face flooded with colour and then paled. He had phrased it all wrong! It was *Steven* who was living with him! Horror grew as she realised with a sort of slow-motion fear just what he had implied.

'I'll come back later.' Gerald Norton's voice sounded utterly unreal and he had to clear his throat. 'Ring down if you need me.'

He only got a brief and indifferent nod. Kyle's grey eyes were on Alexandra. 'I'll see you later too, Alex,' he murmured softly, and she was shocked to notice that the quietly caressing tone was still there, the softened face and the slight smile on those hard lips. He had done this quite deliberately!

She just walked out and Gerald Norton was right there to open the door for her, hideously solicitous. She was quite surprised to find that he simply let her walk away without any nasty comments—surprised, that was, until she realised just what her new position was to him. She was living with Kyle Maddison and that meant only one thing to anyone who had heard it. Gerald Norton wouldn't dare to offend her.

A slow fury grew inside her as she went down to her office. For some reason it suited Kyle Maddison to have people think she was his mistress. He had not given one thought to her feelings or her reputation. How could it help with Aunt Cora? Surely he realised that Cora Kent was strictly old-fashioned? She would be shocked out of her mind. She *had* been shocked out of her mind! It had even silenced her.

Janey was still waiting by the lift and Eliot was there too. He carefully did not look at her but Janey was looking at her oddly, she noticed, and they didn't even know about the latest bombshell. She closed her office door and marched about fuming. She should have stayed there and raved at Kyle on the spot. It was just that he had this ability to take her breath away. She contemplated going back and having it out with him right then and there, but she knew really that she hadn't sufficient control of her shaky feelings to count on being any sort of adversary for that cold, bright intelligence.

A whole hour passed and she simply wasted it, looking up cagily from time to time as footsteps passed her office. Nobody came in and she realised that she hadn't the nerve to go down to the foyer at all. How was she going to face everyone? When Aunt Cora came past her door she recognised the brisk footsteps and they didn't pause, although she knew quite well where Alexandra was. Her reputation was down at zero as far as Cora Kent was concerned. She only hoped that Kyle's was too; not that he would care—he had a masterful disregard for the opinions of anyone else.

He let her stew for another hour and then he came himself, calmly walking into her office and leaving the door wide open. 'It's lunchtime.'

His grey eyes were intent but not at all apologetic, and she opened her mouth to make her opinions known and then realised that anyone close by would hear. The only positive action she could take was to look at him with intense dislike, and he infuriated her further by smiling that superior smile that seemed to come from some hidden core of wickedness.

'I can see you've been wasting your valuable time,' he murmured, his eyes moving over her empty desk. 'I have something more productive for you to do after lunch. Meanwhile, as I said, it's lunchtime. Let's go!'

She took that to be an invitation to lunch and sat quite still with no intention of moving until he took one step closer, looking very dangerous.

'Alexandra!'

There was no smile of any description and her defiance drained away as she remembered his previous method of punishment—remembered too the threat about Steven. For now he had her securely at a disadvantage, but she looked at him with eyes that threatened and the cold gaze that held hers recognised it.

They went to Zucco's and Alexandra flinched as she realised just where they were going. 'This is not my kind of place!'

The sharp sound of her voice was the only sound he had heard from her since they had walked out of the building past Janey's interested eyes. Eliot had just been crossing the foyer too as they had left, and she'd sensed the same speculating appraisal from him. He would know soon enough—they all would—fear of Kyle would not keep Gerald Norton quiet. This was a piece of gossip too good to waste.

'This is where successful businessmen eat their lunch,' he assured her. 'There won't be a single yuppie in here, if that's what's worrying you. The place will be full of middle-aged businessmen worrying about their affairs and their ulcers.'

'They'll have more to worry about when you step through the door,' she remarked bitterly. 'There'll be a stampede to get out.'

'I do not conduct my business affairs over lunch.'

'Ah. They don't know that, do they? Every time you accidentally look at someone they'll imagine that their firm is for the chopping-block.'

'I'm beginning to wonder if you enjoyed being punished,' he murmured quietly as he ushered her through the doors. 'Don't forget who I am, please. Surely you realise that the presence of a room full of spectators would not in any way deter me if you go too far? You must know by now that I don't give a damn what others think.'

As a threat it was superb, she had to admit that. It silenced her completely and she noticed too that many of the men there looked up and nodded cheerfully to Kyle. There were few women, but it seemed that every one of them brightened up as he walked in. Alexandra felt very conspicuous and found herself moving closer to Kyle as the waiter led them to a corner table.

'I suppose that bringing me here is your idea of a joke,' she muttered angrily.

'I thought you needed a good lunch,' he said innocently. 'I can't imagine why you're so uptight. You are most certainly the most beautiful woman here. Any one of them would give a fortune to have your hair and that little-girl look that seems to be constantly surfacing.'

'I'm not a little girl,' Alexandra seethed quietly as the waiter left them to choose from the menu. 'I did not want to have lunch with you even though I can see that you feel guilty enough to bring me out to a smart place. A few minutes alone in your office would have been much more to my liking!'

'Really? The punishment *did* impress you, didn't it?' His mouth twisted ironically. 'Later, Alexandra. If you're very good, I'll see what I can do.' As far as she was concerned that was the end of any conversation and her decision seemed to bother Kyle not at all—he simply ate his meal.

In the end it was Alexandra who gave in.

'Why did you do it?' she asked miserably. 'What have I ever done to you to make this necessary? Just a few words and you've ruined my reputation.'

'Do you really care so much?' He looked up at her slowly, the grey eyes roaming over her face. 'It wasn't quite what I intended, but the opportunity was so easy to grasp and I'm really an expert at grasping opportunities. Even so, does it matter so much in these days?'

'It matters to me!' Alexandra looked up at him with angry eyes. 'I'll have to explain to everyone and then they'll know about Steven.'

'I think not!' The hard, cold look was right back where it usually rested, in those chilling eyes. 'There will be no explanations. You assured me when we first met that you had no particular desire to remain with Fosdick-Kent. You can resign. Other factors will of course remain the same. If you desert the ship then Steven goes back to court. If you can't face people thinking that you're living with me then simply leave. I'm quite capable of keeping you. I assure you that you'll want for nothing at all and there is the added advantage that you'll be able to keep an eye on your brother during the day. All in all it's not such a bad idea.'

'No way!' For the moment Alexandra quite forgot where they were and didn't much care who heard. If this was stage two of any strategy then he could think again.

'If you have the nerve to pretend that I'm living with you, then so have I! It gives me certain advantages, not the least being that I can speak to you any way I like. Secondly, I'll have the satisfaction of knowing that your little meanness has lost you Aunt Cora's shares for all time. She's the original old-fashioned aunt, Mr Maddison. She does not approve of modern values and now you can be quite sure that she doesn't approve of you! It really doesn't matter to me; she'll not feel like interfering again with my life now I'm a lost cause.'

He looked at her steadily, the moment stretching out until his cold eyes became very unnerving. 'I have more tricks up my sleeve than you could possibly imagine,' he said when her eyes finally fell before the cold stare. 'I don't just "do" things, Miss Kent. I plan things.'

Her new-found defiance began to ebb away and they went right back to silence, a state of affairs that he clearly much preferred.

It was like waking up and finding that the nightmare was actually happening, Alexandra thought. It dawned on her outraged mind too that the trip out to lunch was also deliberate, and she was quite annoyed to realise that she had not thought of that straight away. Not only was Kyle Maddison allowing people to imagine that she was living with him, he was actively encouraging the idea.

As they walked into the offices after lunch, Janey moved guiltily round the back of her desk, but it was clear she had been telling people that Alexandra was out at lunch with the boss. The person who was now being enlightened was Eliot, and to Alexandra's shame he did not move away guiltily or otherwise. He stood there with an expression on his face that told her clearly he had also received information from Gerald Norton.

'Get the latest accounts for me, Alex,' Kyle murmured with a smile that infuriated her. 'Come straight up with them.'

His expression and tone told her exactly what he was doing. He was throwing her into Eliot's company at once and she had no idea what to say. For one wild moment she thought of asking Kyle to wait for her, but he was already at the lift and his curt nod to an unsmiling Eliot reminded her that she had thrown Eliot to this particular wolf when she had pretended that he was her boyfriend. She wasn't about to drag him in deeper.

'Kyle wants the latest accounts.' She could have bitten her tongue as the words came out. She had got used to thinking of that monster as Kyle!

'I heard.' Eliot's face was stiff and he simply turned to walk to his office, leaving her to walk behind or run to catch up with him. Quite clearly he was in possession of what he imagined were facts.

'Here they are.' He already had them in his hand as she reached his office door and he avoided her eyes quite deliberately.

'Eliot,' she began, not quite knowing what she was going to say but unable to just leave things as they were. It wasn't that Eliot meant anything to her particularly but he must be feeling very deceived and, after all, he was a friend—at least, he had been a friend until Kyle had come so disastrously into her life.

'Did you know him before he came here?' Eliot asked tightly and it quite surprised her. Evidently he had been mulling things over while she had lunch.

'Of course not!'

It wasn't an answer that pleased him and she assumed she had said quite the wrong thing.

'He's a fast worker, then, but still, we know that, don't we? What astounds me is that he was able to get you into bed with such speed. I only gave you a goodnight kiss and I had the feeling that I was close to rape as far as you were concerned. I can see you were saving yourself for something better!'

Normally he would have got a direct attack for words like that, but she understood how he felt and she was so very shocked and vulnerable herself, her life having been taken out of her hands.

'You don't understand . . .' she began, realising as she said it that she was unable to give an explanation. Kyle had sewn up every outlet. She couldn't see any escape route at all.

'I'm thirty and perfectly normal,' he snapped. 'I understand what "living with" someone means! I'm surprised he allows you to work. He doesn't need to count the pennies. He could easily keep you.'

He could. He had already said that. It was what they all expected next, but Kyle had been that one jump ahead as usual. Why was he doing this to her? Why? She was just standing there, staring blankly at Eliot, and he turned away in disgust.

'You'd better get back up there, Alex, before he comes down to fetch you,' he muttered, and there was nothing she could do but turn away. Kyle might just do that anyway. She felt sick inside and, as she stood at the lift, Janey avoided her eyes. Normally they chatted whenever Alexandra was down here. She liked Janey. She had been going to invite her home one evening.

Kyle looked at her intently as she walked into his office. She hadn't bothered to knock and she knew that for a second the fact had annoyed him, but now he just looked at her and said nothing. She put the papers on his desk and her own phone began to ring—she could hear it through the open door. It was a good excuse to hurry off and gain a few minutes.

It was Aunt Cora. She had reached home and had been thinking. That was quite clear.

'I've never been so ashamed, so humiliated in my life,' she began in her most righteous voice. 'If your mother had been alive she would have felt exactly as I do! When

I think of how you've turned out after all the good up-bringing you had. I imagined that Steven was the black sheep of the family but quite clearly you're the same. I certainly do not want to speak to you again, Alexandra. I just wish you had another name. You've sullied the name of Kent. Everyone is going to know, so don't think it can be kept secret. What that man does is usually in the papers. You'll be next, your name splashed about for all to see!'

She slammed the phone down before Alexandra could even say one word. And what could she say anyhow? Oh, you don't understand, Aunt Cora, Steven would probably have gone to prison and Kyle made me live with him so I could share the responsibility. I'm not living with him really, though. If she did that, Kyle would throw Steven out and back to that starchy magistrate.

It wasn't true about her mother, either. Her mother would have been here to give Kyle Maddison a piece of her mind. The thought of her mother brought tears to her eyes, brought the whole past back. It was true that Steven had been spoiled, but it hadn't meant she had been loved less. He had only been spoiled after he had become ill. Things had been happy, though. She hadn't been alone.

She had never felt so alone as she did now. Steven would be back at Downham Manor, his nose under the bonnet of a vintage car, not a care in the world, and meanwhile she was here, listening to tirades like that, having to take the scorn that Eliot had heaped on her, and there was no way out that she could see without abandoning Steven. She couldn't do that.

She walked back to Kyle's office, her cheeks still red from the words that Cora Kent had thrown at her. At the moment she didn't feel she had much fight left in her.

'Who was that?' He was watching her as usual but she avoided his eyes.

'Nothing. It was personal.'

'The last personal call you had led us into deep trouble,' he remarked, bracketing them both together as if he had every right.

'Don't worry. We know where Steven is. This is my own problem!'

'If it's Davis . . .' he began, but she looked up wildly, her voice raised.

'It's not Eliot. I've already had my talking-to from him, thank you!' She turned away wretchedly, utterly lost for one moment. It couldn't be happening to her. He had turned her whole life upside-down. 'I don't suppose it will be the last, either. I—I don't live in a vacuum, you know. People know me. Even—even the woman next door will be wondering, the whole street speculating about where I am. They're going to know soon enough when this gets into the papers.' Her last words were choked. She could barely get them out and he came round the desk, taking her shoulders in a hard grip.

'Who the hell said anything about putting this in the newspapers?' he rasped, his aggression reaching her through his hard fingers.

'Aunt Cora! She—she said you're always in the papers and my name will be s-splashed around too because—because I'm l-living with you.'

'You're not living with me. You're simply staying at my house.'

'Try explaining that to them,' she cried bitterly, turning on him. 'Try telling anyone that. You *said* it, after all! You said it to Aunt Cora and Gerald Norton was right there!'

'I don't give a damn what anyone thinks!' he ground out and it was just about the last straw.

'I do.' She dropped her head and burst into tears. It was all too much. Months of worry and trouble with Steven, overworked and tired since Kyle had come here, and now this. Punishment of the worst kind when she had done nothing at all. 'I didn't *do* anything,' she sobbed. 'You—you've turned me into a—a——'

'Don't say it,' he warned fiercely. 'I haven't turned you into anything. You were already knee-deep into an affair with Davis. What difference does it make if people think you've changed your affections to me?'

It was so callous that it stopped her grief and she looked up at him, tears and anger sparkling in her eyes. 'The difference is that I enjoyed going out with Eliot. If I want to have an affair I'll choose the man myself and not in a million years would I choose you. You've—you've sneaked into my life!'

'I don't do much in the way of sneaking,' he grated, his hands tightening on her slender shoulders. 'I take what I want very openly. As far as you're concerned, I think a little co-operation would be wise.'

It was menacing and it reminded her forcefully of her predicament. Tears were not about to influence Kyle Maddison.

'So I'm to pretend that we're living together?' she asked, white-lipped.

'Until it suits me to state otherwise.' His grip softened and he looked a little less alarming. 'You have no need for all this grief. I thought you were made of tougher material but, after all, you're just scared.'

'I'm not! I'm just furious!'

'I promise you it will all come out right,' he murmured, looking into her eyes, fingers soothing her shoulders.

'You can't promise that. You can't give back a reputation once it's gone.' She looked up at him with accusing eyes. 'My reputation is finished here and finished everywhere when this gets out!'

'You're the first woman to get annoyed at the idea of being my mistress,' he said with callous amusement. 'Normally they queue up for the privilege.'

'Then get out and glance along the queue! I'm not fitted for the part!'

'Yes, you are,' he informed her coolly. 'You are Alexandra Kent. I did warn you that you were necessary for my plans when I took this place over.'

'You didn't take me over!' Alexandra stormed, red-faced.

'Have I tried?' he queried sardonically, looking down at her furious face. 'If I decided to try...'

She just went on looking at him and his head came down slowly as if he knew his eyes were mesmerising her. His fingers tilted her face and his lips closed over hers gently. It was so soothing that she did not struggle, and he drew her slowly closer until they were pressed together. And it was comfortable, warm. His lips teased at hers until her mouth opened and his tongue feathered along her lips before he let the kiss deepen.

Every single thought had left her mind. It was like being in a trance. Her body was strange, listening for him in some odd way, and she deepened the kiss even further herself until his hand cupped her head, holding it to his, his lips draining her of all the anxieties that had brought on the tears.

She dimly heard the knock on the door and the hasty, 'Sorry!' and the sound of another voice pulled her out of the cloud to gaze up at him in bewilderment.

'It was only Ian,' he assured her softly. 'He's gone out again.'

He didn't care at all, he was still holding her, his eyes on the softness of her lips, and she came to life with shocking speed. Only Ian! He was probably used to seeing this sort of thing working so close to Kyle Maddison, the queue of mistresses stretching on endlessly.

Alexandra pulled away and turned her back to him, trying desperately to return to normal. 'I'm a real fool, aren't I?' she exclaimed bitterly. 'I step carefully into the web, one foot at a time and then stand here and succumb to the most despicable thing of all, sexual coercion!'

He spun her round, his hand hard on her chin, the grey eyes blazing with anger. For one moment she thought he was going to shake her or worse, but he struggled and contained that violent rage that seared through him. 'Did I hear you say you're taking your car home tonight?' he rasped, his hand tightening even further.

'Y-yes.' She was too shattered to do much raging herself now.

'Then get your coat, get your car and leave!' he snapped.

He let her go and she was only too glad to leave, but she hadn't quite got to the door before his voice hit her, crackling with anger.

'Remember which home you're going to, Alexandra! Don't forget that you live with me!'

She almost ran out and she was still trembling as she backed her car out of the underground garage and drove out into the traffic. He seemed to have given her the afternoon off, even if it had been done violently. Automatically she turned for her own house. There were one or two things she wanted to do. Even before she got there, though, she knew she couldn't do it. Mrs Nash always came out as she heard the car—she seemed to have nothing to do but spy and gossip. Alexandra couldn't face it. She turned for the motorway and Downham Manor. It was the only refuge she had at the moment. Tears of frustration came back into her eyes but she bit on her lip and made her mind up. She couldn't continue to face this, not even for Steven. She would get there at once and have a talk with him, explain everything. She would ring up Aunt Cora too, and Eliot.

Even before she got there and turned into the beautiful parkland she knew it wasn't possible, though. A ruthless man with grey eyes would fling Steven back to court and say just what he liked. Even if she blurted out the whole unlikely story, who would people believe? She didn't have to think much about that. They would believe Kyle and he would be without mercy. He was a raider, after all. He had stalked into her life, grasping opportunities, and had made life unbearable.

She didn't feel like going into the garage to face Steven at the moment but, as she entered the hall, Graves met her, his face tight with annoyance.

'Is Mr Maddison with you, Miss Kent?' he asked quietly enough, although she knew he was fuming about something.

'Er—no, Graves. He—he gave me the afternoon off.'

'Then I'm very glad, Miss Kent, because I have no quarrel with you at all and Mr Maddison has a very uncertain temper. When he finds out...'

Steven! It had to be! Her heart sank even further as she simply looked at Graves and waited for the inevitable announcement, for the blow to fall. It had all happened before. She should be quite used to it by now, but she never would be.

'This morning, Miss Kent, some—friends of your brother's arrived. They arrived on motorcycles and behaved very badly. There was nothing I could do about it and finally they left. Your brother left with them.'

He stopped and she could see that he was really very upset as well as annoyed.

'You mean they actually came into the house?'

'Yes, Miss Kent. They refused to go. Apparently they thought the whole thing was very amusing. They intimated that I too was very amusing.'

She could imagine the things they had said and she felt a swift burst of rage. How dared Steven invite his weird friends to this house? She was suffering all this and he was just going on as normal, if it was normal to go about with those uncouth louts. Graves was shaking and she felt guilty as she had never felt before. He was a nice man, an old man, used to dignity.

'What did Steven do?' She didn't really need to ask.

'Very little to help, Miss Kent. Finally he left with them, as I say, but he didn't look too upset about it all.'

No, he wouldn't. Steven just left everyone else to be upset.

'I'll deal with it, Graves. I'm very sorry, but you can leave it to me.'

'They're not little boys, Miss Kent,' he said with a worried look at her. 'They looked quite tough. I must say I cannot understand how your brother knows people like that. He's not really the same as they are.'

Oh, yes, he was. If Steven weren't like that then he would not have anything to do with them. She was filled with fury against just about everyone in the world, and that included Steven.

'Don't worry about me, Graves,' she said tightly. 'They'll be a lot smaller when I meet them.'

She was still riding a wave of white-hot rage as she pulled up in her street behind a line of carelessly parked motorbikes. Steven had never brought them home before. She didn't even know what they looked like, but she could guess. Far from changing Steven for the better, it seemed that the luxury of Downham Manor had made him feel above any kind of reproof.

She exploded into the house, too enraged to worry that the hall was filled with leather-clad youths. 'Out!'

Alexandra left the door open and pointed at it with a look on her face that left them in no doubt about their welcome. Her fury seemed to have them at a disadvantage. Three of them left looking slightly sheepish; the fourth, however, called her a name that left her speechless. That was when Steven also exploded, and she was still standing shocked and unbelieving when he closed the door with a bang on the last of them.

'You invited them here, to our house——!' Alexandra began, but he stopped her angrily.

'Why not? It's my house too. I'm a prisoner up there with his lordship. It's fine. I like the cars and I like working on them, but I'm not going to be trapped.'

Trapped? She was the one who was trapped. Nothing had changed with Steven.

'So you just went off with them. You didn't care that I would have to pick up the pieces?'

'I never thought about it,' Steven said, a little abashed. 'You don't have to nursemaid me.'

'I do! If it weren't for Kyle you'd be behind bars and after this he'll probably see to it that you are. Meanwhile I'm stuck at the manor for no good reason except that you're there!'

She was shouting at him as she had never done before. This day had been a real nightmare, and this was the last straw. He looked at her uneasily.

'I'll make you a cup of tea before we set off home, Sis.'

It shocked her into staring at him wildly, her temper forgotten for a moment. '*This* is our home!'

'It doesn't much feel like it, does it?' he asked glumly as he went to the kitchen. 'Home is where the boss is.'

She still went on staring at the door he had just walked through. What would their lives be like when Kyle let them go? It would all end and they would be back here, Kyle gone. She looked around slowly at the things that had been so familiar to her. Already they seemed distant, empty. She too was sinking into Kyle's life—no, he was dragging her into it for reasons of his own. It made her miserable. It made her feel more vulnerable than ever.

This business with Steven had momentarily driven her own problems out of her mind and now they swung back again. She *had* to manage Steven by herself. She had to get them both away from Kyle somehow.

The doorbell began to ring rather viciously and, before she could move, Steven was at the door, his face now a little grim. It was Kyle, and he just ignored Steven. His eyes went straight to Alexandra's face.

'Is this a planned escape or a spur-of-the-moment thing?' he asked quietly, his grey eyes punishingly intent. 'I imagine that I'd made it quite plain that——'

'She came to get me.'

Steven's interruption was quite brave, Alexandra thought, in view of Kyle's quietly boiling rage.

'And how did you get here?' Kyle wanted to know, the cold eyes turning on Steven, who looked like a boy again in spite of his prompt action in tossing out the youth who had sworn at Alexandra.

'Back of a bike. I didn't move your cars, Mr Maddison.' Kyle just looked at him and he added hastily, 'I was just making Alex a cup of tea. She's had a shock.'

'Nothing to compare with the shock you will have if you ever again allow your dubious friends to approach my house,' Kyle said menacingly. 'You will behave as *I* expect you to behave. You will follow orders until orders are no longer necessary. Do I make myself clear?'

Steven's head seemed to be unable to stop nodding, and Kyle turned to Alexandra.

'There's tea at home,' he said firmly, taking her arm and urging her to her feet, and Steven looked ready to agree with anything.

'This is home,' Alexandra said bitterly, but low enough so that only Kyle heard as Steven hurried to switch off the kettle.

'But not for you, not for some considerable time to come,' Kyle warned grimly in an equally low voice. 'Get into my car.'

'I'm taking my own car back!' She jerked her arm away and stood there quite ready to make a scene.

'Very well. When I pull into the drive, though, I'll expect to see you right behind me. If I have to turn out again tonight I'll be slightly annoyed.'

He looked threatening, and Steven got his word in very quickly as he came in at the tail-end of the exchange.

'I'll go with Alex.'

They both got a very keen look and Kyle stood by impatiently as Steven locked the door and followed Alexandra to her car. They were back where they had started the day, Kyle's prisoners. Steven knew it too, but he did not know the whole story. Alexandra prayed he would never have to find out.

CHAPTER FIVE

'HE'S annoyed.' Steven's observation as soon as Kyle was out of hearing-distance only irritated Alexandra further. She didn't bother to reply. Why should she? She was being herded back. She was even driving herself there. She couldn't think of even one happy thought and darkly, at the back of her mind, rose the memory of how she had felt when Kyle had kissed her so gently.

'This engine sounds a bit ropy,' Steven muttered after listening for a second or two. 'I'll have to have a look at it.'

She was somewhat taken aback, snapped right into the present. This was new. He had never offered to do one thing for her ever, and he was definitely worried about the sound of the car. 'I imagine you've got enough work to keep you busy with the Bugatti, providing you can manage to stay put.'

'It's nothing that can't wait,' he grumbled. 'Anyway, if I step out of line again Kyle will think of something unpleasant to teach me a lesson. He looks as if it wouldn't take much thought either. I don't want you to drive this again until I've had a look at it, though. There's a certain sound that gives me a very uneasy feeling. Drive slowly now.'

'It's all right.' The concern in his voice suddenly made her feel better. Maybe he cared. Maybe somebody was concerned about her.

Steven looked across at her impatiently. 'Who's supposed to be the expert?' he snapped. 'Go with Kyle tomorrow and I'll get around to the car during the day.'

There was a difference in him after all, even though he had broken away to his old habits this once. Could it be that he was growing up, or was it Kyle? Kyle was so powerful a personality himself that it washed off on everyone around him—it swamped her! He would be a very good example for any impressionable young man, better than the weird, uncouth friends that Steven had always had.

Being close to Kyle might alter Steven's whole life. She nibbled at her bottom lip thoughtfully, sinking her own desires for Steven. Somehow she would have to stick this out.

Dinner was a very subdued meal when they got back. Graves was still very deeply annoyed and Kyle's eyes were frequently on Alexandra, as if he thought she had tried to run off and take Steven with her, even though he must have had the story from Graves to have been there so speedily.

'There's something wrong with Alex's car,' Steven said abruptly towards the end of the meal. 'I've asked her not to drive it until I can get a look at it.' He avoided Kyle's eyes but, now the threat had been made and they were both safely back at the Downham Manor, Kyle seemed able to ignore the whole episode.

'Right. We don't want any accidents.' He seemed barely interested, but he spoke to Alexandra later as Steven went up to his room. 'Tomorrow you'll go with me. Steven can give the car a going-over during the day.'

'Do you want me to come tomorrow?'

'I do.' He looked at her impatiently. 'In any case, I have not forgotten your remarks on the subject of simply staying at home.'

'It's not my home,' she snapped, glaring up at him with dark eyes.

'While you're living with me it is,' he derided, adding, as she looked likely to explode, 'It's the shareholders' meeting tomorrow in any case. You have to be there.'

'Why?' Her voice was belligerent but he ignored that.

'Because I want you there,' he murmured, walking over to her. 'Don't try doing my job again either,' he added as he stood and looked down at her. 'Graves phoned the office to tell me what happened, and I might add that he told me only because he was sure you would be savagely beaten up. Don't go flying off like that again. I take care of Steven—you're merely the referee.'

'I managed perfectly well,' Alexandra muttered, avoiding his eyes, 'and there was no need whatever to come and herd me back here—we were coming.'

'I came to protect you, child,' he said sardonically. 'I expected to have to demolish a rowdy gang.'

'There were only four and—and Steven wasn't just going off really.'

'Oh, naturally not,' he sneered. 'Never mind. You're back here now. Graves will get around to forgiving you both, you'll go on making excuses for baby brother and we'll just go on as normal.'

'There's nothing normal about you!' Alexandra snapped, and the usual hard finger came to tilt her defiant face.

'How would you know? You don't know me from Adam.' He smiled strangely, making her heart thud. 'You're going to know me, though, finally. You're going to know me very well indeed, Alexandra.'

Kyle conducted the shareholders' meeting rather differently from her Uncle Bob's way, Alexandra mused as she set out the papers in the small but splendid boardroom. She had done this plenty of times before, but according to Kyle's orders it seemed that there would be more present than she was used to. Gerald Norton was going to be here for one thing, and then there was Ian Jagger and Carruthers, first name unknown. She wondered how the shareholders would take to this full-house situation.

Kyle had been very cool this morning. She had come in to work with him and had seen various eyes turn in their direction as the Ferrari had growled its way to the underground garage. They had come up in the lift together too, another fact that had escaped no one. She would have to face it, but it was gnawing away at her all the time. She didn't quite have that sort of cool defiance that would have made this unusual situation easy to handle.

She was horrified later when she saw Aunt Cora arrive. After the tirade she had received by telephone she was certain that Cora Kent would not wish to even set foot in the building, but she came and Alexandra dived into her own office. She might have known. Nobody could silence Cora. If there was a meeting she was going to speak at it and nothing was going to stop her.

The door to her office opened and Kyle stood there, tall and intimidating. 'We're ready to begin,' he informed her coldly. 'As far as I can tell everyone is here, so let's get to the meeting.'

She looked at him helplessly, wanting to beg for a reprieve, but he showed no sign of any compassion. He knew why she wanted to back out of it and he was not at all sympathetic. She stood up and gathered her notebook and he politely ushered her out in front of him; at least, it must have been politeness but Alexandra felt as if he was standing behind her so that she couldn't make a run for it.

A quick glance round assured her that as far as the majority of the people in the room were concerned she was no more important than she had ever been. She got one or two polite nods but Cora Kent kept her face averted, her expression icy. Gerald Norton didn't look away—his eyes were gleaming with malicious pleasure and he looked at her in a way he had never dared to do before.

His glance said volumes. She was nothing special after all, she had moved in with the boss. If he had been wealthy enough she would have moved in with him. Alexandra's face flushed painfully and Kyle shot her an exasperated glance. It was all right for him. He hadn't seen the look and he wouldn't have cared if he had.

Things proceeded fairly well. Alexandra relaxed a little as she sat by Kyle and took notes. Ian Jagger was taking notes too and so was the mysterious Carruthers, for some reason she couldn't fathom. It was then that Cora had her say.

'Next to the new chairman, I imagine I'm the major shareholder?' she said acidly.

'It would appear so.' Kyle spoke quietly and Alexandra saw the looks passed between the others. Cora was about to launch into sound—they were quite accustomed to it.

'I believe you're still interested in acquiring my shares, Mr Maddison?'

'I've made no secret of that, Mrs Kent,' he murmured with some amusement. Cora was not amused. Her eyes swept contemptuously over Alexandra.

'I've decided to sell to you.' She looked across at him malevolently. 'I had intended to keep them. My husband started this firm, built it up and made its name well respected. The Kent name has always been respected.'

'I assure you the name will stay and continue to be respected, Mrs Kent,' Kyle said with less good humour. 'I had not envisaged changing it.'

'My conditions for a sale will be that the name *is* changed. You have plenty of other companies, Mr Maddison. You seem to do exactly as you wish. If you want my shares then alter the name of this company!'

Alexandra knew why, and she wanted to run out before Cora could say anything else.

'You have a good reason, I imagine?' Kyle looked at her coolly. 'You seem to have had a sudden change of heart about the shares too.'

'Quite sudden! I never intended to sell, as you know very well. However, I cannot continue to attend meetings when someone who bears my name is sitting here as bold as brass. I had not for one moment imagined when I refused to sell that my own niece would become your mistress! Naturally I want nothing more to do with the firm. You may make an offer for the shares at your convenience.'

Alexandra was too humiliated to even move at all, and Cora swept to the door while the air almost hummed with embarrassed silence. Kyle's voice, thick with anger, stopped Cora in her tracks.

'It's convenient now, Mrs Kent,' he rasped icily. 'That being the case, I'll make my offer at once. Present market value and a decision this minute!'

Cora's face slowly coloured to an ugly red as she met the icy grey eyes. His whole demeanour was threatening. She would never again be able to come here and hold forth, the bit between her teeth, and she recognised it almost audibly. 'I accept!' She spun round and walked out and Kyle stood perfectly still for one second, visibly controlling a violent rage. Even so, his voice was back to being darkly quiet when he spoke.

'I think, gentlemen, that after that small bombshell we should close the meeting.'

There were murmurs of consent and everyone hastily gathered their papers, trying not to look anywhere else. Alexandra was too stunned to react. Never in her life had she faced public humiliation and she sat staring blankly in front of her. It took a few seconds before Kyle's words to Cora Kent began to sink in and with them came a terrifying feeling. She was to be the whipping-boy for everything.

Kyle took her arm and drew her to her feet and she noticed that Ian Jagger had not left the room either. Just the three of them were there.

'Shall I deal with the shares now?' Ian Jagger began, his eyebrows raised, and she seemed to see him for the first time. He looked clever, extremely clever, but then he would be, as he was so close to Kyle. He had a crop of short-cut fair hair, thickly curling. His spectacles were big and impressive-looking. She must be shocked, to linger on such things when her life had been just laid out for all to see.

Kyle looked at him and nodded grimly. 'You do. Right now! Now that I've got her, she's not wriggling off the hook. I want my hand completely closed around this firm by morning!'

There was a sort of amused satisfaction on Ian Jagger's face and Alexandra looked at Kyle in a dazed way as he led her back to his office. Those two were so attuned to each other's cunning ways that they needed no words apparently. Did Ian Jagger know that she was being sacrificed for these shares? Was he kept up to date with everything?

Kyle walked straight to the drinks cabinet and poured her a brandy. It had the effect of bringing her to life. It also seemed to sharpen her mind.

'You planned all this right from the first, didn't you?' she accused hotly. 'You knew how she would react and you just drew me into the net. I was so pleased with myself to tell you that Aunt Cora would never sell now she thought I was living with you, but that's exactly what you wanted. You predicted her reaction. That's why you wanted me there today as well. You knew she couldn't sit there in the same room and not have a go at me!'

He moved the brandy glass from her hand and then took her shoulders and shook her hard. It was unexpected and shocking.

'Like hell I did!' he glared at her. 'I may be foxy, but people like Cora Kent are utterly outside my experience! You imagine I knew that your brother was going to steal a car and wreck it? Maybe you think I put him up to it?'

'I wouldn't put anything past you!' Alexandra shouted. 'I've been publicly humiliated, but what does it matter? You've got the rest of the shares. Another successful deal completed!'

'Oh, I can deal with almost anything,' he murmured, her rage not getting to him at all as his own rage subsided.

'If you do anything it will be for yourself,' Alexandra stormed. 'She humiliated you too!'

'Innocent little fool,' he taunted, his eyes utterly derisive. 'You imagine I'm humiliated that everyone there thought a beautiful girl had moved so quickly into my bed? No man is going to quibble at that, it's what most men boast about even when it hasn't happened.' He walked away, danger in every line of his body. 'I have plans for dealing with Cora Kent,' he said quietly. 'It's time the board had a good laugh. Some of them are quite old—they've had to listen to her for a very long time, after all.'

'What do you mean?' she asked worriedly, the fight dying as other feelings took its place.

'I'm not at all accustomed to such scenes. Normally, private affairs are kept out of the boardroom—they're kept out of my boardrooms at any rate. I'll deal with Cora.'

She just stared at him and he walked across to her, tilting her chin imperiously.

'I'm a bad enemy, Alex,' he assured her quietly. 'Remember that!'

She escaped to her own office and he let her go. She wasn't hiding—she told herself that very firmly, but inside she knew she had run for cover, hidden herself in her own hole, cowered to lick her wounds. There was no kind of escape. Wherever her mind turned there was the same thing looking at her. She was branded as Kyle Maddison's mistress, a girl who had speedily and wantonly moved in with him. People would be speculating now as to what had been going on when she had been forced to work such late hours when he had first come here, work done in a quiet dark building when she and Kyle had been the only two people left there.

She suddenly realised that he had probably thought of that too; in fact he most certainly would have. She was such a fool! All the time she had been bitterly complaining and resenting the loss of her free evenings, he had been planning to make her lose her freedom and reputation—because she had no sort of freedom, that was clear. Wherever she went there would be eyes watching, fingers pointing.

In desperation she began to organise the minutes of the board meeting and then stopped as she realised she had no idea what to put. Did she mention Aunt Cora's outburst? Did she miss it out? She imagined the minutes being read out at the next meeting, Cora Kent's words all down in black and white. Hysteria bubbled up inside her and she nearly jumped out of her skin when she looked up to find Gerald Norton standing in her doorway watching her with sly speculation.

'What do you want?' Her hands were so shaky that she clenched them in her lap, well below the desk where he could see nothing at all.

'I'm just getting a good look at a "gold-digger", Miss Butter-wouldn't-melt-in-her-mouth, who leapt into bed with the first millionaire she saw. Has he got anything going for him besides money? Does he manage to melt that cool exterior better than Davis did? I hear that Davis didn't get quite that far, or did he?'

'Get out of here!' Alexandra stood on shaking legs and stared at him white-faced, but his oily smile simply grew.

'I'm the general manager, don't forget. You may be mistress in the bedroom but here you're just a secretary. Maybe when Maddison moves on and leaves you behind, I'll do a take-over myself.'

Alexandra didn't have time to even think of a reply. Kyle was suddenly there, towering over Gerald Norton, his eyes icily grey.

'You wanted to see me, Norton?'

'Er—no. I was just having a word with——'

'My secretary is too busy to gossip. If it's important send her a memo in the usual way.' He stood perfectly still as Gerald Norton moved away red-faced, and then Kyle added, his voice cold and harsh, 'Which reminds me. I want to see you—tomorrow will do.'

The tone of his voice said that tomorrow was not going to be a good day and Alexandra saw Gerald Norton stiffen, his face now as white as hers as he went down to the lift, heading for his own office.

Kyle spun round to Alexandra, his brows in a black frown. 'What did he want?'

'He—he was gossiping, as you said. He——'

'Don't lie to me, Alex! I heard enough to get the general drift of the conversation, and the way you look now I wouldn't have even had to hear that much.'

'How do you expect me to look?' Alexandra asked, her eyes wide and accusing, almost black with misery, her face haunted.

'Exactly as you do look, I expect,' he said briefly. 'There's little I can do this minute, but after the weekend you'll not have to see Norton again.'

'You can't sack him!' Alexandra cried anxiously. She stared at him, not knowing how hunted she looked. Everyone who spoke against her was about to be savagely punished, it seemed, but it was Kyle who had made it all happen.

'I can move him,' Kyle told her shortly, his face grim as he looked at her pale cheeks. 'Tomorrow he gets a choice: move or be redundant. I really don't need a general manager. I manage very well all by myself,' he added with a sardonic smile.

Only too well, she thought, staring at him bitterly, and he glanced down at the papers in his hand, his smile fading as if it had never been there at all.

'Get these down to accounts and tell that receptionist that I have an important visitor due soon, a Mr Constantine. She is to show him up with no delay and none of her usual self-important preening—phrase that order exactly as you like!'

He turned and walked back to his office, banging the door, and Alexandra steeled herself for a journey to accounts and the foyer and a head-on conversation with Janey.

In accounts nobody paid any attention to her except to take the papers and say thank you. Eliot didn't even look up, although he heard her voice. She was an outcast in her own place of work, sent to Coventry for doing nothing at all except care about her brother.

Janey just looked at her glassily and nodded, even though Alexandra used none of the pithy words that Kyle had suggested.

'The three of you will be having a small cocktail party when Mr Constantine comes, I expect?' Janey murmured sarcastically as Alexandra turned to go, and it was the last straw. Alexandra's temper flared to white heat, her shock of earlier submerged in rage.

'Not at all likely,' she snapped. 'Kyle and I do our celebrating at home!'

'I'm sure I don't care at all what you do!' Janey retaliated, but Alexandra was in full swing and nothing was about to stop her.

'Don't you? Tell me, would the whole building be shocked out of its collective small mind if I was sleeping with Eliot Davis? Is my moral tone the thing that's offending everyone or is it the fact that Kyle is wealthy? Is this a sort of peculiar inverted snobbery?'

'Nobody cares,' Janey began, her face red and flustered at this head-on attack when she had expected blushes and shame.

'Then pass the word that they can mind their own business,' Alexandra raged, 'and if they're so outraged that I'm living with Kyle then let them come up to the main office and voice their displeasure to the boss!'

She stopped as Janey's face went from red to white and back to red again. Her eyes were no longer on Alexandra, and as Alexandra turned her head she saw the lift standing open and Kyle in it, his expression one of narrow-eyed speculation. He punched the button and simply went back up to his office, but his eyes were on Alexandra until the doors closed. She was reminded of the first time she had seen him, those grey eyes on her constantly. Was that when he had picked her out for her present position as scapegoat? He probably had! She marched across the foyer to the lift and followed him up.

She half expected him to be waiting for her, but he wasn't. There was no doubt that he had heard almost every word she had said, but even now she was too enraged to be at all anxious about what he thought. She pulled the typewriter towards her and began to do the minutes.

He just appeared, silently and sardonically, and stood leaning in the doorway, his hand in one pocket, his powerful shoulder against the door-frame. 'Keeping yourself occupied, I see?' The deep, dark voice was edged with amusement, but Alexandra was not amused.

'I'm doing the minutes. I wanted a word with you about them too. There's a difficulty. What am I to write when I get to Aunt Cora's outburst?' She assumed a cool, efficient voice and looked at the blank paper in front of her. 'Mrs Kent offered to sell her shares to the chairman, informing him that she would not be able to attend further board meetings as his seduction of her niece did not meet with her approval. She invited him to get in touch with her when he was prepared to make an offer. At this point the chairman offered to buy the shares and suggested that the meeting be closed. The board agreed and left with red faces.' Alexandra looked up at him with furious eyes. 'Would that be an accurate account of the minutes, do you think, Mr Maddison?'

Annoyance and amusement fought a battle on his face but amusement won and his flashing smile almost devastated her. Not quite, though—she was too angry.

'Your eyes are like black pansies,' he noted, his smile growing. 'I'm pleased to see that you're back on form, insubordinate.'

'It's just not possible to be insubordinate to someone when you're their mistress,' Alexandra snapped—unwisely.

'But you're not my mistress, Alex,' he reminded her softly. 'In spite of your angry words in the foyer, we both know why you're staying at my house. However, if you have any plans, let me know. I did ask you once to let me know when you wanted to be devoured. Just say the word.'

He turned and left, and Alexandra's rage died as other more subtle feelings took over. She was becoming more enmeshed every day, more committed to a lie with everything she said. Why had he done this wicked thing? She almost went back to tears, but he had acquired this habit of creeping up on her recently and she wouldn't give him the satisfaction of seeing how upset she was. He might hold her again and that was not a good idea either. Her pale face flushed and she cast the minutes aside, determined to cross that particular bridge when she came to it. She had plenty of other things to do even though at this moment she couldn't stop thinking about that smile and the seductive words spoken in that velvet voice.

She managed to get through the day, dreading the ride home, but Kyle was utterly silent. She cast a cautious look at him as they drove out of London and he looked extremely complacent. It would be wrong to say he looked smug. She couldn't even begin to imagine Kyle Maddison looking smug; that was a small feeling, well beneath his imperious power. He looked satisfied and calm, like a predator who had herded the prey into a corner with no way out. There was even a slight smile edging his lips if she looked closely.

She looked away hastily. If Kyle was calmly satisfied then somebody was about to be devastated. Why did she always feel that it was going to be her? It was probably nothing to do with her at all. He moved with savage speed when he was after something, that much she had learned before she had ever seen him. There had been a visitor, and although she hadn't seen the mysterious Mr Constantine she knew he had been. Maybe Kyle was up to something in a new direction? She very carefully relaxed.

It wasn't a good idea—she found that out after dinner. There was the usual talk of cars. Apparently the Bugatti was about to cost Kyle a small fortune. Steven had a preliminary list of its requirements and he looked a bit anxious as he and Kyle pored over it like two surgeons, but Kyle took it all in his stride and even seemed eager to visit the 'man down by the docks' to get the parts made.

'Can I have a word with you, Alex?' Kyle asked politely after the meal was over and Steven had taken himself off to his room with a book—an entirely new innovation for him.

She could hardly say, 'No, you can't,' and she found herself standing uneasily in his study as he walked to the heavy dark oak desk and leaned on it, his face quite matter-of-fact as he dropped his latest bombshell.

'I had Constantine in my office today,' he reminded her. 'You know who he is?' She shook her head, her eyes almost mesmerised by his cool, arrogant face.

'He has a small press agency. They dish out interesting items to the dailies. He does very well as he never gives them a wrong tip. He gets his information at source, straight from the horse's mouth, as they say.' He paused and looked at her levelly, his voice bland. 'I announced our engagement. It will be in tomorrow's papers.'

Alexandra had thought that after the last few days nothing at all could shock her. How wrong could she be? She simply gaped at him, too astounded to have any feeling at all except sheer incredulity. It was quite a few seconds before it hit her and he waited calmly, his grey eyes cool and alert on her face.

'What? You've done what?' Her voice rose almost hysterically and he moved quickly, grasping her arms, ready to shake her again, no doubt.

'You heard me perfectly well,' he rasped. 'Lower that voice, Alexandra, or we'll have Steven here to rescue you.'

'Rescue me? Nobody can rescue me. I'm drowning in meanness, wickedness, lies...' He shook her then, gently but with enough force to make her realise he could pick her up with one hand and shake her perfectly well like that.

'Be sensible! It's the best thing to do. It covers all avenues——'

'You mean it cuts off all retreats!' She pulled free and spun away from him, heading for the door, throwing her remarks over her shoulder. 'I'll ring up every paper and tell them that if they print I'll sue!'

He reached forward and swept her right off her feet, holding her against his chest, his eyes furious as he glared at her, and then he strode to the huge leather settee and almost threw her down, sitting beside her, his arms pinning her before she could move or get her breath back.

'I half expected this,' he grated, glaring down at her, his eyes punishingly cold. 'You imagine I'm about to let Cora Kent get away with her display of this morning? If you remember, she pointed out to you that it would be in all the papers. Well, it *will* be in all the papers, but not quite what she expects. Tomorrow we announce our engagement and we have a celebration dinner to display the ring. You mourned the loss of your respectability. I'm giving it back to you.'

'You took it away in the first place,' she reminded him hotly. 'You sacrificed me to get Aunt Cora's shares, and when you've tied up the firm and moved on I'll have to live with the people here.'

'What makes you think I'm moving on?' He was immediately alert, watchful, and her heart gave a peculiar leap as she suddenly saw him again as she had seen him when he had first stalked into her life—an intelligence, bright and shining, a man to be feared.

'Gerald Norton said——'

'I heard something of what Norton said,' he growled, the watchful look in his eyes partially replaced by anger. 'As from Monday he'll be spreading rumours in Nottingham.'

'I don't care!' She moved fretfully, trapped by powerful arms that had come down on either side of her, looking up into his strong, unyielding face. 'I don't need anyone to tell me that you'll move on. Our firm is small, insignificant. You have a business empire. I know you only want the land.'

'Do you?' he murmured thoughtfully, his eyes roaming over her face. 'Well, let's just say that for the time being I'm taking a breather before going back to the fray.'

That was rich. The fray had never stopped since he'd come into her life. He just brushed it off as a game to keep his hand in trim. His gaze was piercingly grey, like a menacing sea.

'I'm not about to throw you to the wolves, pansy-eyes.'

'I'm never going to meet a bigger wolf than you in my whole life,' she said gamely, her mind anxiously wondering how long she could outface him, and he smiled down at her disturbingly.

'As the wolf is protecting your brother and trying to rescue your reputation, how about a little co-operation—in the matter of this engagement,' he added derisively as her face flushed and her spirited looks turned to anxiety. 'If you promise to behave nicely, I'll let you get up.'

'I'm not making any promises to you!' she snapped. 'Whatever I do you'll turn to your own advantage. I'll fight you all the way.'

'Oh, well, then . . .' He lifted her into his arms and the cool, scornful lips covered her own.

Alexandra struggled, although she was in a position that gave her no advantage whatever, but he simply tightened his grip, his laughter mocking against her mouth.

'Don't fight me, Alex,' he advised softly. 'You're never going to win and, after all, I have every right to kiss you—we're engaged.'

CHAPTER SIX

ALEXANDRA'S fierce denial was cut off by the pressure of Kyle's mouth, and after a second she completely forgot that there was any sort of conflict. He was warm, safe, comfortable. Everything was so right, so natural. It was impossible to stop herself from relaxing, from winding her arms around his neck, and she was completely lost in the kiss as he lowered her to the cushions, his hand cupping her face as he turned her further towards him.

If he had said anything, anything at all, she would have come to her senses, but he said nothing. His lips never left hers. They were fused together, his arms just holding her safely until excitement grew inside her to an altogether alien pitch. Waves of feeling spread through her body, each wave more strong than the next, and she gave a little whimper that was part anxiety and part frustration.

Then he touched her, his hand moving to her breast to mould it softly, and her breathing seemed to be suddenly suspended as a great tide of response engulfed her, her whole world shot by stars.

'Kyle!'

'You're safe, Alex,' he murmured against her mouth. 'There's nothing to be afraid of. Wanting somebody is perfectly normal.'

It wasn't. Not when it was the man who had ruined your reputation and probably your life. But she ignored the stern voice that pointed this out. It was more wonderful to listen to Kyle's dark, velvet voice and she moaned softly, coiling against him as his hand moved beneath her sweater to push her lacy bra aside and close over her breast.

She wanted to touch him too, to caress the man who had turned her life upside-down, and her fingers clenched in the dark, crisp hair, her hand moving behind his bent head to touch the strong muscles of his neck and urge him closer.

'Alex!' His voice was muffled against her neck, his teeth beginning to make gentle bites at her skin. 'It's only fair to warn you that I want you too.'

'You're never fair,' she groaned, arching against his caresses. 'You wouldn't know how to be fair.'

'Wouldn't I?' he asked fiercely. 'You don't know me at all!'

'I don't want to know you.'

Her words seemed to drive him out of control and he pulled the sweater over her head, tossing it to the floor, his eyes raking over the swift rise and fall of her breasts before the clip of her bra snapped open beneath his fingers and he buried his face against her, his mouth moving to capture one sharp pink nub and caress it hotly.

'No!'

It was no protest but a gasp of pained rapture and he recognised it for what it was, his hands tightening on her slender waist and lifting her closer to his demanding lips.

When he finally let her sink back to the cushions, his hand covered the throbbing silk of her breast as his lips moved to her waist and the trembling planes of her stomach.

'You know me better now, Alex,' he murmured thickly, his face against her pale skin. 'You know what I want too. Not many people can say that.' He lifted his head and blazing silvery eyes looked at her. 'Tomorrow you'll be engaged to me. In the morning you'll go into London and buy yourself a gown for the evening, a gown that will stop all speculation about the reality of this engagement. You'll charge it to me, then there'll be no doubt about it. In the evening you'll have the ring and we celebrate.'

He lifted her up, ignoring the shattering effect his lovemaking had had on her. He found her bra and fastened the clip, his face taut and relentless, and then he was pulling the sweater back over her head, guiding her arms into it as if she were a rag doll, straightening it and smoothing her hair. He even looped the strands behind her ears as he had seen her do so often.

Only then did he sit up straight and look at her again before he pulled her to her feet, letting her stand on trembling legs.

'I'll tell you one last thing,' he said harshly. 'When Constantine came to my office it was not at my invitation. He rang me for an interview. I told you he gets his information at source and he was checking for tomorrow's press release. It wasn't much, just a snippet. "Kyle Maddison's latest mistress—latest take-over." Cora Kent was right, you see. It was going to be splashed all over the press. Now it reads, "Business tycoon engaged. Kyle Maddison to marry the niece of the late Bob Kent." Which do you prefer, Alex?'

Alexandra couldn't answer him. She just stood looking at him with wide dark eyes, her body trembling almost uncontrollably after his passionate onslaught, and he turned away impatiently, his strong face harsh in the lamplight.

'Go to bed!' he grated savagely. 'You now know as much as I do, including the fact that we want each other.'

She didn't dare to argue with that. It was all too clear, blindingly obvious. She turned and almost stumbled to the door, aching all over, inside and out, and frightened as she had never been.

It was only as she reached her room and began to shakily undress that one phrase rang over and over in her brain. 'Kyle Maddison's latest mistress.' Latest! That part had never been in any doubt—he had even told her about the women who queued up, glamorous women, Dulcie Hepworth merely one of the many. A searing wave of jealousy hit her and she almost fell into bed, to lie trembling and shamed until it was almost dawn.

Alexandra felt more than trapped as she sat beside Kyle to go to work on the following day. Her life had been taken over with a speed that even now left her dazed. More than that, though, during the long night she had faced the feelings that had been growing for some time. The shock of recognition when she had first come to the house and felt the magnetism that reached out to her when Kyle was there was now a permanent part of her life. She had been mesmerised almost from her first sight of him, but she had never envisaged anything like the feelings she had now.

She kept silent, her face determinedly turned away from his, and he seemed to be quite content to leave things like that. He had said no more to her than a polite good morning, and she faced the day with the realisation that the newspapers would be delivered even before they reached London and the office.

They had been. The whole building seemed to be throbbing although there was nobody there in the foyer but Janey. It was an atmosphere, something in the air, and she needed no confirmation other than the way Janey's eyes looked. She was remembering the way she had spoken to Alexandra, the way she had ignored her with the rest of the office staff, and now she was uneasy about it. Alexandra was part of Kyle Maddison's life—official—and Janey's anxious way of trying to catch Alexandra's eyes verified it all.

Kyle was way above it even if he noticed. He was not a man to concern himself with the anxieties of others. He expected people to be anxious when he was around, and the only difference in his behaviour was that he took Alexandra's arm firmly and possessively as he walked across the foyer with her.

'I say! Congratulations!'

Ian Jagger's face was wreathed in smiles as they entered Kyle's office, and to Alexandra's surprise he looked totally genuine. Of course he was a very pleasant young man in spite of his close contact with Kyle, and he obviously thought this was all real.

She tried to smile but her eyes were glassy, her cheeks flushed with much more than embarrassment. She wanted this to be real. The thought hit her unexpectedly and she wanted to run to her office and hide.

'Thanks, Ian. A friendly face at this time is a welcome sight,' Kyle murmured with an impatient sidelong glance at Alexandra's distressed face. 'You'll have a bit of extra work this morning, though. Alexandra has to go out for a while and I want you to take her jobs under your wing for a few hours. There'll be calls about our engagement too, I expect. Deal with them, will you?'

'Already have,' Ian said with one of his pleasant grins. 'There have been calls from the afternoon editions to verify the announcement, a few private calls that I've listed for you to deal with and—er—Mrs Kent called for Miss Kent.'

'Call her Alexandra,' Kyle murmured. 'She's one of the family now and, speaking of the family, I'll deal with Aunt Cora. Route her calls to me. Alex is not to be bothered.'

As Ian left with a cheery grin at her, Alexandra stood like a dutiful slave waiting for orders and Kyle's smiles died as the door closed behind his private secretary.

'The dress,' he said briefly. 'Go out and buy it. You have all morning, all day if necessary. Just see to it that when this evening comes you're ready to face the world as my fiancée, looking like my fiancée,' he added coolly. 'Don't forget that you charge it to me. I wouldn't want this little drama to cost you anything. We've restored your reputation. I wouldn't want you to have to pay for the subterfuge.'

She just turned and walked out. It was all beginning to hurt rather too much, and when she finally left her office and went down to the foyer to head for the street she was almost numb inside.

'Alexandra?' Janey called to her and she stopped politely, her face utterly without expression.

'I just wanted to say congratulations.'

Janey was red-faced, but Alexandra didn't feel like helping her out at all. She just nodded and walked out. She had her own miseries to cope with. Janey's were self-inflicted.

A taxi glided up as she stepped through the door. 'Miss Kent? I'm to take you into the city and stay with you as long as you need me.'

Alexandra got in, icy-faced. The feeling of being encircled was complete—she wasn't even to be allowed to roam at will. She wondered if the taxi driver had been instructed to see that she didn't go to any cheap shops? She leaned forward and spoke coldly, giving him the name of her bank and the street. She might be trapped in more ways than one, but she had no intention of being bought and paid for.

Alexandra drew out almost everything she had left, ignoring the rather scandalised looks of the cashier. He wanted an expensive drama? She would show him. She ordered the driver to take her to Bond Street, imitating Kyle's regal manner, and he was much impressed. Alexandra sat back and fumed.

*   *   *

'It's you,' the assistant said, stepping back to look admiringly at Alexandra. 'As soon as you walked through the door I envisaged you in this creation.' It was a very good line in buttering-up customers but Alexandra looked at herself in the mirror and had to agree. The long deep blue dress suited her to perfection. In fact, it did more than that. It almost changed her appearance entirely. The contrast with the fair shine of her hair, her pale skin, made her look almost unreal and her heart gave an almost painful thump as she imagined Kyle looking at her in this dress.

She had hardly stopped thinking about him since last night and her earlier annoyance had faded, anxiety taking its place as she wondered where this celebration was to take place, who would be there. She took a shuddering breath and said she would have the dress, and the accessories that were pressed on her.

She was hardly back in the changing-room before a new customer entered the shop, and even in there she could feel the atmosphere. She soon found out why.

'Why, Miss Hepwarth! Your gown is ready. It only needed the slightest bit of alteration.'

Alexandra stiffened with shock. Dulcie Hepwarth was right out there in the salon. She couldn't go out and face her! There had been a photograph of both Kyle and herself in the morning editions.

'Well, I don't normally buy things "off the peg", but this quite took my eye. Let's hope I'm not disappointed.'

The rather throaty voice was just a little threatening and Dulcie didn't stay long to chatter. She had left the impression that all this was beneath her, and there was a murmur of resentment as she left.

'If her fans knew what she was *really* like...'

'Maybe she's seen the morning papers? She wasn't quite like that when she came in here before, and everybody knew she was going to marry Kyle Maddison.'

'Everybody *thought* they knew! Apparently he doesn't stick to one woman for very long.' There were several titters of laughter and then the curtains of the booth were pulled open and Alexandra found herself facing the woman who had served her.

'Are you all right, madam? You seemed to be such a long time.'

'My zip was stuck,' Alexandra improvised quickly, hoping that struggles with a zip could explain her flushed face. Apparently it did and she escaped into the street, closing the door firmly as she heard,

'Isn't that the girl in the morning's papers? The one who's the latest?'

'Don't be silly, she's too ordinary. Kyle Maddison goes for glamour. You've just had a close look at Dulcie Hepworth—what do you think?'

Alexandra was glad of the waiting taxi. She sank back in the seat trembling. What a mess! Her hands clenched together as she realised she had been jealous again in there, jealous at the sound of Dulcie Hepworth's voice. 'He doesn't stick to one woman for very long.' Those words too rang round in her head. She wasn't even in that category. She closed her eyes with a sigh, preparing to face the rest of the day and Kyle.

There was nothing to face. Her desk was empty, and when she summoned enough courage to go to Kyle's office he looked up coldly as she knocked and walked in.

'What am I to do?' She stood uneasily as he glared at her. 'I—I'm back.'

'There's nothing to do at all,' he growled, looking back at his own desk that was overflowing with work, picking up his pen and getting on as if she weren't there at all. 'Paint your nails,' he continued sardonically, 'or you could simply hide. You're getting quite good at that.'

'Shall—shall I help you?' she asked anxiously, too nervous with him now to show any fight.

'Thank you, no!' he bit out without even looking up.

It annoyed her. It was so unfair. He was angry and she had done nothing at all except get herself into this mess and obey his orders like a simpleton. 'Why are you so annoyed with *me*?' she snapped, her dark eyes sparking purple lights.

The grey, coldly intelligent eyes looked up at her, although he did not even raise his head. 'For the same reason that people climb mountains,' he rasped. 'Because you're there!'

Alexandra spun round to leave, her face pale. He could hurt her now. He had done all this to her and now he could hurt her badly. She wasn't going to let him find out. She wasn't going to let it happen again.

'And in future,' he added icily, 'when you come to my office, you do not knock. You're my fiancée. Act the part—the affectionate smile, the lingering look——'

'I never attempt things that are beyond my capabilities!' Alexandra snapped, spinning around, her hand on the door. 'You got yourself into this, you can damn well get yourself out of it. Lies and subterfuge are your forte. Count me as a dead weight!'

Kyle's face darkened angrily, his eyes piercingly grey and menacing, but as he half rose from his desk Alexandra walked out and slammed the door. Let him make the best of that! If he came after her with that murderous expression on his face she would shout her head off at him and she didn't care if the whole building heard.

As usual, he was one jump ahead of her. He left her strictly alone and she spent the rest of the day bored out of her mind with plenty of time to just think about him. She couldn't go anywhere without seeing someone who would now be wanting to change their minds and be nice to her. She didn't even have any nail varnish with her to follow his sardonic advice. The day seemed to last for two years.

Alexandra did glean one interesting item of information when Ian Jagger popped into her office later to return some work. By way of small talk he told her that Aunt Cora's telephone call of that morning had been neither to congratulate nor enquire. She had called to complain. Her shares now belonged to Kyle and apparently, in some obscure way, Alexandra was to blame.

What had she expected? she asked herself. Wasn't she taking the punishment for everything? Kyle would now deal with the minutiae, as he had informed her before. He was intelligence in block capitals, ruthlessness in italics. Who could hold out against Kyle?

During the drive back to Downham Manor there was still an air of suppressed ferocity about him, and Alexandra kept silent. She had worries enough as it was, mostly about this evening's supposed celebration. She didn't want to bring Kyle's wrath down on her head unnecessarily. She would need his support.

It appeared that Graves had been told to feed Steven and that they would be dining out, and Steven was not in the garage. He must had heard them arrive because he was hovering around the hall as they went in, an expression on his face that was part-way between a grin and a grimace of anxiety. He just looked like a boy and a very young one at this moment.

'Graves said that you're dining out.' He was looking at Kyle, Alexandra noted, not at her.

'That's right,' Kyle said shortly. 'Sorry, but you're not invited.'

He sounded tightly angry, and Alexandra bristled anew.

'I'm not fishing for an invitation,' Steven said quickly. 'I just wondered... Graves said that... Are you really engaged?' he suddenly burst out.

'We are.' Kyle turned slowly and looked at him with serious grey eyes. 'It was necessary to tell Graves because he takes time to read my paper before he lets me have it. I know his little ways. He's been with the family for a long time. I thought you'd be too engrossed with the Bugatti to find out. I was going to tell you myself. I didn't quite know how you would take it, you and Alexandra being so close.'

'Oh, boy!' There was not much doubt about how he was going to take it. He hugged Alexandra in a burst of delight and Kyle simply nodded gravely and went up the wide stairs, no doubt disgusted with them both.

'All our worries are over, Alex!' Steven said excitedly. 'He's rolling in money. Imagine having him for a brother-in-law! Kyle Maddison! Wow!'

Wow, indeed. Alexandra's smile was very shaky as she made her escape to her room to prepare for this—celebration. All Steven thought about apparently was easy living. This was the latest of Kyle's sins. She had not for one moment imagined that Steven would have to be told. It was ridiculous, but she had somehow thought of herself and Kyle as being in a world apart from her other life. Now it was touching Steven. When the end came he would be let down, disappointed, angry. He might even go back to being the person he had been before, and all this sacrifice she was making would have been for nothing at all.

She showered and stood for simply ages at the mirror, brushing her hair with no real thought behind it, her mind on other things, miserable things. It was an effort to dress for going out and only the thought of Kyle's anger prevented her from locking herself in her room, getting into bed and shouting from there that she had a headache when Kyle came hammering on the door. The ensuing row would alert Steven. It was better to pretend for his sake, while it was possible to go on pretending. She felt halfway between tears and rage and the sight of herself in the beautiful, wickedly expensive dress only added to the feeling of unreality that had grown in her during the weeks she had known Kyle.

This was not her. This girl with hair that shone like silk in the lights, with a pearly skin and eyes that looked too big for her face, was not Alexandra Kent. She had no idea where Alexandra Kent had gone, had little hope of getting her back because even if she should suddenly wake and find that this was all a dream she would never really recover from knowing Kyle. She would never have been able to recover from even having simply dreamed about him.

He came when she was standing looking at herself forlornly, coming into her room when she answered despondently as he knocked. She had thought it would be Steven with more congratulations, and as Kyle walked in she just stood and looked at him with no time to change her expression.

He stopped, his glance moving over her from her shining hair to her bewildered expression and the dark eyes that looked haunted and lost.

'I brought the ring.' His eyes lanced over her again, lingering on her smooth shoulders, narrow waist and the full skirt of the deep blue dress. The chiffon seemed to drift around her and he walked forward slowly, taking her suddenly lifeless hand and slipping the ring on to her finger.

'It fits.' He looked down at her slender hand as it still lay in his strong palm and her eyes followed his gaze, her breath catching in her throat at the beauty of the huge diamond that glittered in the light, all the colours of the rainbow reflected on its perfect surface.

'It's beautiful.' She could only whisper and couldn't move her hand away, but he let it go, turning aside, his shoulders lifted in a dismissive shrug.

'I'm glad you don't think it's ostentatious. It had to be big to show easily tonight.' His lips twisted ironically. 'I'm even wearing a dark dinner-jacket so that it will show against my arm. Be sure to keep your hand on my sleeve as we dance.'

He turned and walked out, and Alexandra moved to the dressing-table to put on her necklace and add the finishing touches for the evening. She was lost between tears and anxiety, not knowing where he was about to take her for people to see, hurt by his indifference even if it was all so many lies.

He walked back in as she stood to survey the final touch, and this time he didn't even knock. 'You can take the beads off,' he said abruptly, his voice harsh. 'Beads are not the thing to wear where we're going.'

This time she felt sparks rising inside her, her eyes flashing back to life as she turned on him. 'They're not beads!' she snapped. 'They're rhinestones and really quite expensive.'

'They clash with the real thing,' he told her bitingly. 'The dress needs pearls and these are real.' He opened a black velvet box and took out a string of milk-white pearls that had a glow of their own.

'I'm not wearing anything of yours!' She stepped back as he made to fasten them around her neck. 'I may have to wear the ring but I'm not wearing anything else.'

'What about the dress?' he asked derisively, his eyes glittering with anger although his voice was back to deep, velvet mockery.

'I paid for it with my own money.' She raised her chin defiantly and met his piercing grey gaze. 'I would have bought it myself if it had taken every penny I possessed!' It *had* taken every penny she possessed—well, almost—but there was no way he was going to find out.

'You look like Steven when he's been up to no good,' he informed her sarcastically. 'However, we'll call the pearls an engagement present.'

Before she could stop him he had removed her necklace and was fastening the pearls around her throat, his fingers frighteningly warm and relaxing against her skin. It only made her fight more. She was not going to get close to him again—not ever.

Her hand came to tear them off and he caught it, holding it tightly.

'Damage these and you'll be repaying me for about a thousand years,' he warned angrily. 'If they bother you, you can give them back with the ring when your reputation is well established as sound and untarnished and this whole thing is over.'

She pulled free of his grasp and turned away, her silky hair hiding her face. 'And what about Steven?' she asked bitterly. 'Do we throw him back to the past, tell him it was all a slick manoeuvre to get Aunt Cora's shares and now it's all over? How many other lives have you wrecked?'

'Whose life are you most concerned about, yours or Steven's?' he asked quietly, with none of the anger she had expected considering his mood all through the day. 'How far will you go, how many sacrifices will you make to keep that boy from facing the harsh world? Are you so busy being the little mother that everything else is submerged, including your own desires and dreams?'

'I wasn't making any sacrifices until you stormed into my life.'

He took her shoulders and turned her, but she stood with bowed head and he forced her to face him easily by tilting her chin, capturing her reluctant gaze as she looked up.

'You've been making sacrifices since your parents died,' he reminded her softly. 'And I don't need spies to find that out. I only have to talk to Steven to hear about what you've done. Alex is the greatest! When Steven stays out until three and four she waits up. When Steven wrecks her car she simply pays for the repairs. When Steven gets into trouble she sells almost all her shares and lets him keep his. You were wrecking your life and Steven's long before you met me, Alexandra.'

'I wasn't!' Tears came into her eyes at last, falling like small raindrops to her cheeks, and he muttered under his breath, drawing her into his arms and bringing her head gently to his shoulder.

'Don't,' he said softly, his hand stroking her shining hair. He lifted her face, his hand cupping her cheek as his lips met hers. 'My poor little Alex,' he murmured.

She had never intended that he should be allowed to kiss her ever again, she was sure of that, but as his lips met hers her mind and her body forgot. She felt the peace and strength of him enclosing her and all her fears were simply vanquished as he deepened the kiss and folded her closely against him. It lasted a long time, until she was drifting on a dreamy cloud with no worries at all, and when he lifted his head to look down at her she couldn't even open her eyes.

'I think that's as far as we should go for now,' he said mockingly when her eyes at last managed to open. 'We have our engagement to celebrate in public and I want you to stay as beautiful-looking as you are now. If you want to continue when we get back, just let me know. For now, however, you look much more like a newly engaged girl than you did when I came in here. Perhaps I do have the golden touch after all—as far as you're concerned. Be downstairs in two minutes.'

He walked out and left her standing there and she came slowly to her senses. Tricks! Tricks! Tricks! His whole life was made up of tricks and there was nothing real, warm or human about him. Even his warmth and comfort were unreal, practised strategies to dupe lesser mortals, and she was a lesser mortal. She smoothed her hair and checked her make-up, her face tight with pain and anger. It would never happen again! She winced as she remembered how many times she had said that already.

It was one of the most expensive and exclusive night-spots in London, a place that Alexandra had only read about in the papers, but the doorman knew Kyle and greeted him with a smiling deference that made Alexandra feel more inadequate than ever.

It was not a small corner table for a newly engaged couple, either. The table was on the edge of the dance floor, both of them bathed in bright lights, and she saw Kyle's eyes move to the ring as they settled in their seats, ushered there by a very solicitous head waiter. The ring shone like a beacon. Yes, everyone was going to be quite assured that the announcement was not simply news-paper speculation.

There were plenty of interested people too. As they walked in there had been a slight hush and plenty of eyes both curious and envious had followed them. The envy was from the women and now, as Alexandra risked a furtive glance at Kyle, she could see what they all saw: a handsome, strong face, an air of utter self-assurance, probably the richest and most dangerous man here tonight.

'Why did we have to sit here, right in the lights, where everyone who feels like it can spend the evening watching us?' Alexandra murmured the anxious words as the waiter left Kyle with the wine list and made a discreet withdrawal.

He reached across and captured her fluttering hands, turning the ring to the light and glancing at its glitter. 'I was brought up to face everything head-on,' he informed her quietly, his eyes moving to her pale face. 'My grandfather always impressed upon me that if anything is worth doing at all it's worth doing very well indeed. If it's not worth the effort it should be discarded.'

'This isn't worth the effort,' Alexandra said shakily, making no attempt to move her hands from his warm fingers. It gave her some of the courage she lacked and she knew that she would be discarded very soon.

'If it weren't I wouldn't be doing it,' he said irritably. 'You are my fiancée. This place is a hot-bed of gossip and that's why we're here. Tomorrow anybody who doubted the press will be left in no doubt at all.'

Alexandra was left in no doubt herself of the truth of these remarks. There was a bright flash of light and a quick nod from Kyle gave the photographer permission to do exactly as he liked with the shot he had taken quickly. He would sell it. They would be in tomorrow's papers, this time photographed as a loving couple, Kyle's hand holding hers.

'Relax, Alex,' Kyle ordered softly. 'Just enjoy the evening.'

'There's nothing to enjoy,' she said tremulously and his hands tightened on hers, making her glance up at him.

'There's the fact that you look very beautiful,' he assured her quietly. 'You have no glassy glamour, just a very sweet and bewildered beauty that any woman here would pay thousands for if it were available out of a bottle. They're very busy now wondering where you get your hair done, who did your face. At least laugh at it, you poor little waif.'

It wasn't laughable. She dared not even turn round now and she was very glad when the lights lowered and the floor show began. She didn't even have the nerve to jump up and run out. It was astonishing to think that she had been afraid of Kyle, *should* be afraid of him, but now he was the only person who could make her feel at all courageous. He seemed to have almost stolen her soul.

CHAPTER SEVEN

ALEXANDRA hardly tasted the meal that Kyle ordered and had to admit that he was very patient with her indeed. He was quiet himself, almost as if he was waiting for some momentous happening, and such was her state of nervous tension that when a laughing, chattering party entered as they had almost finished eating every instinct became alert.

They drew attention to themselves, and as she caught sight of the woman who was at the centre of the group Alexandra was not at all surprised when everyone began to clap and get to their feet. It was Dulcie Hepwarth, the present darling of the West End, and her heart sank even further.

Kyle neither clapped nor rose to his feet. He looked sardonically amused at this commotion, and he was still smiling that enigmatic smile when Dulcie Hepwarth turned from her acknowledgement of the tribute to her and saw him. Her face froze, the smile becoming glassy and, to Alexandra's horror, she moved purposefully towards them, her eyes on Kyle but sweeping over Alexandra bitingly.

He stood as she arrived at their table, her entourage left behind, but she waved him to his seat.

'Don't let me interrupt your meal, Kyle,' she said smoothly. 'I just had to come and congratulate you on your engagement. I did think it was all some publicity stunt, but then you never need extra publicity, and here you are with the girl in question.' Her eyes turned on Alexandra and she swept one long, considering look over

114

her. 'Not your type, I would have thought, but then, men don't necessarily marry the same type of person they sleep with, do they?'

Alexandra's face flushed with humiliation but Kyle's lips quirked.

'I would say that they never do,' he murmured ironically, his eyes amused as he watched Dulcie's bitter face. 'Alexandra is sweet and gentle, utterly natural. That's more or less what every man dreams of, even when he's with someone else.'

Dulcie's eyes opened wide, very theatrically. Her make-up was good, Alexandra noted almost in a daze. The eyes were pale blue and heavily made up, quiet startling in these lights, and almost every eye was upon their table. They no doubt saw the tears that Alexandra saw very clearly.

'You're a pig, Kyle,' she whispered. 'Don't expect me to be waiting when you get bored.'

'Oh, I usually know what to expect from you, Dulcie,' Kyle murmured. 'Enjoy your evening. Alexandra and I are going home soon. We don't really care for the bright lights, do we, darling?' He smiled at Alexandra and Dulcie walked off stiffly.

Kyle sat down, a smile twitching the edge of his lips. 'Well, now the main event is over, we'll dance a while and then go home as announced,' he said quietly, his eyes flaring over Alexandra's unhappy face.

'You expected her, didn't you?' she asked bitterly. 'You knew she would come in and that's precisely why we're here.'

He inclined his head slightly in acknowledgement. 'This is where the theatre group come if they are having any success. People come here to see and be seen. I half expected her to come in.'

'You're cruel.' She looked at him in dismay and he shrugged, not at all worried about her opinions.

'If you think so. Don't waste your time feeling sympathy for Dulcie, though. She's an actress and she's acting—rather well, I thought, nothing overstated.'

'She was crying! She didn't look as if she was acting to me,' Alexandra said hotly. She got the same old smile.

'That's why she's a good actress, among other things. In any case,' he added dismissively, 'Dulcie and I have a very special arrangement.' He stood and drew her to her feet. 'Let's dance. It's time for everyone to get one last look at the ring and then we'll go.'

Alexandra was out on the floor before she had really digested that remark. A very special arrangement. She could only think that Dulcie Hepwarth knew all about this pretend engagement and that she was willing to put up with it to get the extra publicity it would give her—the slighted woman. When she got together with Kyle again the whole city would breathe a romantic sigh.

'Hand on the sleeve, Miss Kent,' Kyle ordered mockingly. 'This is the last glitter they get.'

She put her hand there, anger tearing through her at his easy cruelty, and her fingers tightened on his arm, her nails digging into him. He looked down at her, his eyes meeting the angry darkness of hers.

'Getting your claws into me, pansy-eyes?' he taunted.

'You're disgusting!' she fumed, any other feeling swamped by anger.

'Not quite that,' he corrected sardonically. 'I was taken under my grandfather's wing from a very early age and taught to get what I want. He was a very tough old man.'

'He would have to be to let you nestle under his wing. I wouldn't like you under my wing!'

'I'm glad to hear it,' he murmured softly, pulling her close. 'I'd hate it if you wanted to mother me. I'll settle for your just wanting me.'

'I don't!'

He pulled her even closer and cupped her face with one hand, tilting it up to his. 'Tell me that when your eyes don't look quite so bitterly jealous,' he teased gently.

She pulled her face away, but when he moved his hand to her nape to soothe away the tension she was only too glad to put her face against his jacket and hide.

'That's better,' he congratulated softly. 'Let's hope that photographer has his camera ready.'

He did, and as she opened her eyes and saw the flash again Alexandra wondered just how many people Kyle had under his thumb. Every string he pulled worked smoothly. He out-planned and outmanoeuvred everyone. What chance did she have? What chance had she ever had, the sacrificial lamb for Kyle's master plans?

When they arrived home he stood in the quiet hall and looked at her quizzically. 'I realise that you're bursting with indignation. Let's have it now. I wouldn't want you to be up all night seething with rage.'

'You got the shares from Aunt Cora,' Alexandra said tightly. 'She can't back out now, so why this engagement? And don't even bother to tell me that it's to save my reputation because I won't believe you. In any case, I've already lost it and I'll never get it back.'

'Such drama,' he mused tauntingly. 'As to the engagement, it suits me very well. Sometimes a queue of ladies can be very irritating. Odd though it may seem to you, I have other things to do with my life. An engagement will put them off very nicely.'

'If you think that——'

'I think that Steven has served a very small time indeed of his probation with me,' Kyle reminded her coldly. 'You are part of that deal. Six months, Alexandra. It's barely begun. You are also engaged to me so that Cora Kent will suffer embarrassment after her outburst, and never again feel like facing even the most timid member of the board. As things have turned out, she managed to make a fool of herself. So all in all, the engagement is very helpful. It leaves me free to get on with my affairs without the presence of hopeful women and lastly,' he added threateningly, 'it rids us of the necessity of having Davis hanging around.'

'He's not hanging around!' Alexandra glared at him, frustrated and hurt. 'Eliot will never speak to me again.'

'Then he's wiser than he looks. I hope for his sake that he continues to be wise. Six months, Alexandra.'

She found herself facing Eliot much sooner than she had expected. Next morning she met him on her very first trip downstairs. She stiffened with the need to protect herself, but it wasn't at all necessary—not everyone was given to Kyle's sardonic ways. Some people were prepared to say sorry and mean it.

'Don't avoid me, Alex,' Eliot said quietly, his face wryly accepting her reaction. 'I'm really sorry about the way I behaved towards you. I had no right to take my jealousy out on you. I had no right to react like that after only a few dates, either. I know you've had a bad time and I don't want you to go on avoiding me.'

She was so unused to hearing a quiet, simple apology nowadays, so unused to having things utterly straightforward and out in the open, that Alexandra just stood looking at him, almost stunned.

'Alex?' he murmured worriedly and she pulled herself together, managing a smile.

'I think I probably owe you some sort of apology too, Eliot,' she told him softly. 'I—I hope Kyle hasn't been making things awkward for you at all?'

'For me?' He looked at her in surprise and then grinned, quite astonishing her. 'Oh, you're thinking about the Big Creep? I heard that Norton had accepted transfer to Nottingham—in lieu of redundancy. I expect he spoke out of turn?'

'Yes,' Alexandra admitted, red-faced.

'Well, nobody deserved it more,' he remarked. 'As for me, I know when to duck. Apparently Maddison has a mathematical genius with him, so I'm doing my sums twice over.'

'Carruthers,' Alexandra said, suddenly enlightened.

'The same.' He nodded sagely and then smiled. 'It's like old times, chatting away like this. At least we can stay friends, Alex?'

'Of course.' She was so glad, so very glad to have Eliot back as a friend, that she smiled up at him and put her hand on his arm. She was startled when he almost flinched. 'I've got an infectious disease?' she asked, only half joking, and Eliot ducked his head, his smile very weak.

'I don't have a lot of courage surging through my veins, Alex,' he confessed very quietly. 'Not when the boss is watching.'

She turned her head and saw Kyle. He was halfway across the foyer and he had simply stopped, his eyes like steel, biting into her even from there. When she turned around, Eliot had beaten a hasty retreat. No, he didn't have much courage, but at least he was man enough to admit it.

Kyle simply waited, and she despised herself to find that her legs were taking her towards him as if she were mechanically controlled. He ushered her politely into the lift, saying nothing until they had reached their floor, and then not even speaking as they made their way to his office—at least, he made his way there. Alexandra was simply taken along, the usual hand on her arm, not exactly biting but extremely firm.

'Were you arranging to see Davis?' he asked as he closed the door behind them and swung her round. 'When you first came to live with me I said he could take you out from there. That's been cancelled for quite some time now. I expected you to realise that fact. I explained things to you last night. I explained very clearly and very concisely.'

'I was *not* arranging to meet Eliot!' Alexandra snapped, trying to free herself from the iron grip. 'He was merely apologising for being hurt at the way I treated him when I "took up" with you. And I don't live with you,' she added bitterly.

'You live in my house and you're mine!' he rasped. 'That ring proves it!'

'I hate you!' Alexandra raged. 'I hope you can see it in my face because it's true.'

He stood looking down at her, an expression in his eyes that she couldn't even begin to fathom except that it was probably dangerous in view of her outburst of temper. 'I see it in your face, Alex.' The unexpected quiet of his voice startled her. 'I know exactly what you think about me and I accept it. I know you want me too. That's also in your face.'

'It isn't!'

'Oh, yes, it is,' he assured her relentlessly. 'It's not going to go away, either. We're together each day and it will grow. You're mine, Alex. It's right there in your head.'

He lashed his arms around her and searched almost angrily for her lips, tightening her to him with no break even before she had begun to think of struggling. There was no struggle. It was a one-sided contest in any case— Kyle always won. He only had to reach for her and the victory was his. His lips probed deeply, his hand running over her with impatient caresses that vibrated through her whole body.

'I want you,' he said intensely, his words muttered against her lips. 'There's going to be no competition, Alex. You have me or you have nobody at all. I'll crush anyone who even looks at you!'

'You're frightening me,' she managed breathlessly, trying to pull away from the vibrancy of his arms, but she got nowhere at all.

'It's not what I intend,' he murmured, his lips beginning to move over her face and neck. 'I don't want you to be frightened when I hold you.'

The aggressive intensity faded and he began to kiss her slowly and deeply, searching her mouth for endless minutes, his hand cupping her tight breast until she was like some willing toy in his hands, her heart fluttering, her head thrown back wantonly for the heated caresses of his lips.

'That's how I want you to feel when I hold you,' he said thickly. 'That's how you do feel. Admit it, Alex. We're mad about each other.'

Recovering from the frenzy of feeling was not at all easy. She wanted to cling to him, to admit how she felt, but she had her self-respect, even if others thought she didn't. 'You could do that to any woman,' she gasped, straining away from him. 'You've been doing that to me since I first knew you but it doesn't mean a thing except that you're an expert in more than one field. You must have had plenty of other women swooning in your arms,' she added bitterly.

'Countless numbers,' he bit out, letting her go suddenly. 'You're on hand at the moment, though, and while ever this little game is being played, while ever the world thinks we're engaged, I'm somewhat restricted in my activities. As your Aunt Cora pointed out so truly, I'm always in the papers.'

'You can go to Africa,' she snapped, making for the door fast and trying not to look as if she was running away. 'Or Peru,' she added as she made it safely to the door.

'I don't need to,' he said darkly. 'You're here and it's only a matter of time, Alex, isn't it?'

She escaped and almost collapsed in her own office, hoping he wouldn't send for her at all for the rest of the day. It was only his sardonic looks, his sarcastic remarks and his utter indifference towards her feelings that saved her. She knew that perfectly well. If he was ever at all normally kind she would be lost.

When Ian Jagger came walking in later in the afternoon, she was as wary as if he were stalking her for the boss. He was so very disarming, though, and now that she was 'one of the family' he had taken to chatting with her openly. She noted that Kyle did not object to this. Ian was not an unknown factor. He was Kyle's shadow. He had the master's ear in all things.

'You were in this morning's papers. Have you seen them?' Ian asked guilelessly, going on as Alexandra simply shook her head, 'You looked beautiful. Pity it was only black and white. A very handsome couple,' he finished with satisfaction.

'It—it was a bit of a strain,' she confessed and he looked almost laughably sympathetic, very serious.

'I know. I've been with Kyle for almost seven years and I'm only just getting used to the blaze of publicity that follows him around. Mind you, I manage to slide into the shadows. You had the full glare.'

'Seven years?' Alexandra murmured, her eyes startled on his face. 'You don't look old enough.' She had always thought of him as a rather nice young man—well, recently anyway—and he grinned at her expression.

'A matter of genes,' he announced scientifically. 'Runs in the family. I'm more ancient than I look.' He put his head on one side, giving the past some consideration. 'I grew a moustache once, to try to look older. It grew a treat too,' he added, fingering his top lip reminiscently. He grinned. 'Kyle advised its removal. He said it looked as if it needed a lawnmower over it.'

Alexandra found herself laughing, wondering rather sadly what Kyle was like when he was on your side. She would never know that.

'I'm glad about you and Kyle,' Ian said, looking at her levelly. 'He needs someone like you, someone gentle and sweet with just enough spark to stand up to him. I expect he's told you about his grandfather. I only met him twice before he died, but he scared me to death. *There* was a mean, tough man and no question. Kyle's parents were divorced when Kyle was ten and the old man brought him up and left him everything, but there didn't seem to be any gentleness in his character. Kyle must have had a bad time when he was a boy with no other family.'

'There were his parents, even though they were divorced,' Alexandra began, but he shook his head.

'Don't you believe it. They just went their separate ways and he hardly ever saw them. He was left to the mercy of the old man and I should think there wasn't much mercy there. Anyway,' he finished, straightening from his position by her desk, 'he's got you now.'

'And my brother,' Alexandra said quietly, her mind on a very young Kyle with a tough old man to bring him up; no mother, no gentleness.

'I heard,' Ian said, brightening again. 'That's wonderful for Kyle. He's always needed a brother and now he's got one ready-made. He does a lot of work for young people, did you know?' Alexandra shook her head, fascinated by these disclosures, and he nodded sagely. 'No, I expect not. He keeps his good works quiet. The hard image follows him and he's certainly hard when necessary, but I expect you've already discovered his soft side.'

He walked out cheerfully and Alexandra found herself looking at the closed door, her head shaking of its own accord. No, she hadn't discovered his soft side. Helping Steven had been part of a ploy to get Aunt Cora's shares.

That Steven talked to him so much was because of the
cars and the time they spent in the garage together, their
heads under various car bonnets. He hadn't shown any
soft side to her. He had ruthlessly taken her away from
her old life and now he was planning ruthlessly to...
Her mind brought her up with an alarming jolt. She had
to get free of him somehow.

Even so, as they drove home, Kyle silent beside her,
she stole a curious look at him and all she could see was
the strong, handsome face, the capable hands on the
wheel. In her head she could hear the dark velvet of his
voice but her mind saw far away a small boy, lost and
alone, and an old man with a tight face who guided his
steps towards manhood.

Her face softened and she looked abruptly away. Yes,
she did want him, he was right, but it was much more
than that. She would never admit it even to herself, but
he was now a necessary part of her life. It had crept up
on her, unwanted and silently, but it was there, per-
manently there.

She sighed without even knowing it and Kyle's voice
came quietly through the darkness of the car.

'Tired?'

'I—I suppose so.' She kept her face turned away,
feeling very vulnerable at that moment.

'Never mind. Tomorrow is Saturday and you can stay
in bed all day if you like.'

'What will you be doing?' she asked thoughtlessly,
and he laughed softly but made no comment about her
careless remark.

'Steven and I have a date with the "man down by the
docks". It should be very interesting. It will take my
mind away from a very frustrating week. I wonder if he
can make the parts?' he murmured almost to himself
and Alexandra found herself smiling. He sounded then

just like a boy, just like Steven. It was an illusion, she knew that, but somehow she treasured it.

Even in the near-darkness he seemed to pick up her mind-waves. 'Don't mother me, Alex,' he warned quietly. 'That's not what I want from you.'

'You should have been taught that you can't have everything you want,' she retaliated shakily.

'I was taught to take what I wanted and I always have done,' he growled. 'Old habits die hard. Just remember that.'

'I'm not an ailing business venture,' she managed to say firmly. 'I'm a person.'

'You're the woman I want,' he corrected.

'At the moment,' she snapped, stung by his matter-of-fact voice and the way he thought he had only to take anything he desired.

'Isn't that what it's all about,' he jeered, 'one moment after another while it lasts?'

'Some people love each other and it lasts a lifetime,' she said in a tight voice.

'But that's not us, is it, pansy-eyes? What we have is desire and it's just as strong.'

'And lasts no time at all,' she finished bitterly, her voice shaking, try as she would to control it.

'That's life.' Even in the semi-darkness she could see that dismissive shrug and a cold hand seemed to close over her heart. There was no hope with Kyle. Nothing would ever change him. All she could do was bide her time and then escape.

'What are you thinking about?' He stopped the car outside the house and turned to her before she could get out.

'Escape. Only Steven prevents me from going right now.'

'Only Steven brought you here in the first place,' he reminded her quietly, turning her face towards him. 'Live

with me and you won't want to escape at all—I promise.'
He drew her forward. 'Belong to me. I'll make you
happy, Alex, very happy.'

'You're a destroyer! How could you make anyone
happy?'

She pulled free of him and scrambled out, running to
the house and inside before he could move—not that he
hurried to follow her. In her room she sank into a chair
and tried to stop shivering. She wondered about the
young people he helped so quietly. Did he make them
happy? He must do. Steven was changing too, slowly
becoming another person entirely now that Kyle had him
under control. He could never make her happy because
he wanted a moment in her life, an open-ended liaison,
and she wanted something so different: all his love for
all her life. She went into the shower and had a good,
long cry, her face composed and cool when she went
down to dinner.

She was still asleep when they went for the precious spare
parts, but she awoke as they drove off, running to the
window to see Kyle as long as she could. It was a lovely
day and they had taken Kyle's small sports car. She supposed it cost plenty but she knew nothing at all about
cars and all it looked was sporty and fun. They were
chatting as they went down the drive, Steven sitting
beside Kyle, half turned towards him, laughing at something Kyle was saying. She wished she could be like that
with him, just happy and content. He would never allow
it. She was the one who had to make sacrifices all the
time.

She got dressed and went down to breakfast, greeting
Graves with a cheery smile. She wasn't usually so self-
pitying and she wasn't about to start now. He was back
in a few minutes.

'There's a telephone call, Miss Kent. It was for Mr Maddison but as he's out she wants to speak to you.'

'She?' Alexandra looked at him and he nodded.

'Miss Hepwarth,' he murmured, his face giving none of his thoughts away. There was nothing to do but take the call. It crossed her mind to refuse; it also crossed her mind to tell Dulcie Hepwarth that she was merely trapped here, but pride and a ridiculous feeling of loyalty to Kyle kept her silent.

'I assume you're there?' Dulcie snapped when Alexandra just held on to the phone and said nothing. 'You needn't be shy, Miss Kent. It might be a good idea if we got used to the sound of each other's voices, because if you're going to be hanging around there for long you'll certainly be hearing from me. Kyle and I will continue to see each other.'

'Kyle is now engaged——' Alexandra began, but the laughter at the other end of the phone stopped her.

'What did Kyle call you the other night—sweet? Stupid might have been a better description. Kyle and I go back forever. We never part on any permanent basis. The other night was quite startling publicity for me—I was in the papers too. We're turning people away by the hundreds. Exactly the same thing will happen again when Kyle and I get back together. Do try and grow up, Miss Kent. You really are out of your league.'

It was only what Alexandra had worked out for herself. 'What exactly do you want at this moment?' she asked tightly.

'I was going to fix next week's arrangements with Kyle and I couldn't resist a word with you. Anyway, it doesn't matter. He knows his way to my flat, after all, and I expect he'll ring me.'

'I doubt it!' Alexandra snapped, her pride stung badly. There seemed to be no end of the humiliation she was going to suffer and the derisive laughter that lingered in her head as she put the phone down did nothing to help at all.

She put on a jacket and went for a walk to explore the grounds and the nearer lanes, something she had not yet had the time to do. There was a lot of thinking to do, but no amount of thinking could set her free in any way at all. She was trapped because of Steven, and also trapped because she loved Kyle.

The sun was hot but there was a brisk little wind and by the time she turned for home her cheeks were glowing and life didn't seem so very black any more. Maybe something would turn up to alter things.

She had been out for ages and she turned towards the house, stopping and standing aside as a Land Rover came slowly along the lane, coming out into the main road as she stopped to let it pass.

The driver gave her a big smile and drew up, getting out to come and speak to her. 'Are you lost?'

'Not at all. I'm nearly home.' She gave him a smile that was brighter than she felt.

'Home? Oh, what rotten luck! I recognise you now. You're the girl who's engaged to Kyle Maddison. Sorry, I thought I'd found myself a fair maiden.'

Alexandra found herself laughing. He was open and forthright, a good-looking man of about thirty-two, his face tanned and his outfit suggesting that he was a farmer. He also looked quite normal, and normality was something sadly lacking in her life at the moment.

'Grant Wendon,' he introduced. 'I know who you are. I read the item twice with sheer bitterness. I breed horses,' he added when she asked him. 'I've got a place over there.' He pointed to a big house in the distance. 'Actually, you've been trespassing on my land. I turned the Land Rover out to catch you at it but you'd just made it to the Queen's Highway.' He grinned down at her.

'Next time you want to trespass, I'll join you. I'll have the binoculars out every day, just in case.'

He gave her a lift back to the house, chatting easily all the way, and she was just bidding him a smiling goodbye when the small red sports car drew up with a roar behind them. Grant Wendon waved cheerfully to everyone and drove off, but Kyle was not cheerful at all. As Steven went off to the garage with a box of things he handled with great care, Kyle took Alexandra's arm and swung her to face him.

'What did Wendon want?' he snapped, pulling her towards him.

'I was walking and he gave me a lift back,' Alexandra said crossly, annoyed at being treated like a suspicious character.

'Don't encourage him,' he snarled, his face tight with anger. 'If he doesn't know you're engaged to me then I'll soon enlighten him.'

'He knows,' Alexandra said bitterly. 'I should think everyone in the country knows. I'm notorious!'

'No, just desirable,' he murmured, his smile like a tiger. 'Feeling it myself, I recognise it in others. Get involved with Wendon and you'll not have a lot of choice about your future. I'll settle it.'

She stared at him in disbelief and then turned and marched into the house. This was just about the last straw. Not for Steven and not for anybody would she stay here. As soon as she got the chance she would go. She sat down abruptly on the bed as a little sense overrode her annoyance. Go where? If she went back to her own home he would follow. And what about a job? She was stuck with her job at Fosdick-Kent. She had even drawn out her savings, right down to the small change, or almost so.

She sat with her head bent, misery and angry frustration keeping her exactly where she was, and she didn't even hear Kyle come in.

'I'm sorry, Alex.' He walked across and lifted her to her feet, pulling her into his arms even though she struggled. 'Don't fight me, Alex,' he said softly. 'I'm sorry.'

'You're never sorry,' she snapped, trying to turn her head aside, but he cupped her face holding her right where she was.

'With you I am,' he confessed. 'I had no right to speak to you like that. You're not a prisoner.'

'Oh, but I am!' she cried bitterly. 'You've got Steven and I'm stuck with it. I work for you, I've drawn out almost all my money for that dress. What am I but a prisoner?'

'I'll give you anything you want, Alex.' His voice was suddenly velvet-dark again, taut with feeling, and she looked up to find to her surprise that his face was pale. His hands were shaking and she stopped struggling, anxiety taking over from rage.

'What's wrong?' she asked softly, her hand coming to his arm. 'Has anything happened? Are you hurt?'

He turned away, letting her go, his lips twisting sardonically. 'I'm not hurt, not unless you count sexual frustration as an accident.' He shot her a look of annoyance. 'And don't mother me, Alex. Save it for Steven.'

'Oh, I will!' Alexandra snapped, her anxiety for him wiped out at the return to cold sarcasm. 'And on the subject of saving, save your ardour for Dulcie Hepwarth!'

'Meaning what?' He looked at her threateningly but she was filled with anger and bitterness.

'Meaning that she called but you were out. I was the one who took the call. She left a message. She wants to fix next week's arrangements. As you were out she couldn't but, as she pointed out, you know your way to her flat!'

He stared at her for a few seconds, his eyes flaring grey and clear over her flushed face. 'Yes, I know the way to her flat,' he agreed, his eyes narrowed. 'I'll tell her not to call here again. There's no need for you to be upset with things like that. I can just as easily call her.'

He walked out before she could answer and any small hope died right then. She might be keeping off the queue of ladies but Kyle was going right on seeing Dulcie. That would be the next thing in the papers when some snooping journalist saw them. How could she face the humiliation then?

She almost refused to go down to dinner when evening came, but she could have saved herself the trouble. Kyle was out, Graves informed her. He would not be in until very late. She could guess where he was. He had this special understanding with Dulcie Hepwarth and they had to fix up next week's meetings. Dulcie would deal with any frustration he had.

He was still out when she finally went to sleep, too tired and distressed even to cry. She knew deep down that he would be out all night, but she didn't want to have it confirmed.

Next day Alexandra was up early in spite of a miserable night. She could hear nothing at all. Even Graves seemed to be silent and she had the decided feeling that Kyle was not there. He had stayed out all night with Dulcie as she had expected, and the knowledge drove her to a sort of hot mutiny. She ignored breakfast, not even having a cup of tea.

She dressed in jeans and a shirt and went down to the garage for her car. Today she was going home. She couldn't stay there of course, being the hostage she was, but at least she could go and think in her own surroundings, sit and ponder things in the atmosphere she had grown up in. Perhaps a bit of her mother's calm good sense would still be hanging around in the house. She needed it. She needed somebody to hold her hand and tell her what to do.

The keys were in her car and she knew Steven would have finished fixing it. He had sounded so worried that he would have got to it straight away. It sounded just the same to her, just as it had always sounded, but then, she wasn't a mechanical genius. She drove off down the drive and out into the early morning Sunday traffic that was heading out of London. She was taking the other direction and the roads were almost clear. She picked up speed and tried to look at things logically and sensibly.

If she hadn't fallen in love with Kyle, what would she have done at this moment? What would good common sense tell her to do? Get out of there fast. There was no doubt about it. What about Steven, though? She could not see Kyle sending him back to that woman and a spell behind bars, but then, who knew what Kyle would do? He was a man who despised losers, a man who won all the time, who made quite sure that he did, no trick overlooked. It was impossible to even begin to guess what he would do.

There was her job too and her lack of money now, unless she sold the rest of her shares. Kyle would be on to that scheme like a tiger, the shares would be his in no time and he would want to know why she was selling. She sighed. Everywhere she turned there was Kyle, Kyle, Kyle.

She frowned and bit at her lip in frustration, signalling and pulling out into a clear road to overtake a car that was dawdling along as if the driver were pedalling it. She accelerated and was alongside him when a lorry turned into the road from a side road. She had plenty of time to make it and her senses became alert as she put her foot down.

The engine simply died. She could take no action at all, neither forward nor sideways. Her car stopped of its own accord in the wrong lane, the lorry hurtling towards her. She could see the car beside her frantically trying to get clear and he made it, but the lorry was almost upon her and only at the very last minute did she hear the sound of airbrakes being applied.

She threw her arm across her face automatically and the lorry almost managed to stop, the shock of the impact quite slight considering the terrible position she had been in. Even so, her head snapped back, cracking into the headrest, and her world was swimming with nausea and flashing lights before she blacked out.

Everything was hazy. There seemed to be a lot of people there very quickly but she was not even in control of her own legs and opening her eyes hurt enormously. She couldn't answer when questions were asked and she felt hands lifting her out, the sound of an ambulance coming to a stop bringing momentary silence around her, and then she was speeding away smoothly, glad to rest her head on a soft pillow.

CHAPTER EIGHT

IT WAS late in the afternoon before Alexandra really knew what was happening. She had a distant memory of long corridors, of doctors, the quiet of a room with white walls and then nothing at all.

Now she opened her eyes, not really believing it when she saw Kyle and Steven there, both of them standing by her bed, Steven's face chalk-white.

'She's come round. You can have a few minutes.'

A nurse was there too and Alexandra's eyes moved from one to the other, the effort to move them making her wince. She struggled to sit up, but a cool hand came to her shoulder.

'Don't move at all. You're quite all right but you must stay still for a while or you'll have a bad headache. You've had an injection but it's wearing off now.' The nurse nodded at her visitors and then left, her orders making Alexandra sink back to the pillows.

'Are you all right, Sis?' Steven came round Kyle and leaned over the bed. 'We couldn't find you. We thought you were still in bed until it was almost lunchtime, but then I went to the garage and found your car missing. I was scared.' He was twisting his hands together and they were shaking and she looked at him in a sort of wonder. He really loved her. Somehow she had missed that fact for a long time. It had always seemed that he loved himself better than anyone. She wasn't really so smart after all.

'I'm all right.' It was surprising how weak her voice sounded, but the sound of it gave Steven the necessary courage to take her to task.

'I *told* you not to use that car, Alex,' he remonstrated quietly. 'I told you it was ropy. Why did you do it? Do you think I don't know what I'm talking about?'

'I thought you'd done it already,' she whispered, distressed by his pale face.

'I couldn't! It needed parts. Kyle and I brought them back yesterday when we went down to the docks and I was all set to get it done today. It's a miracle you weren't killed and it would have been my fault!'

'Not now, Steven,' Kyle said firmly as tears filled Alexandra's eyes, and Steven saw them too, his face moving from one distress to another.

'I'm sorry, Alex. Just take care. I'll wait outside, you'll want to be alone with Kyle.'

She wanted to cling on to Steven and tell him to stay, but he thoroughly believed this engagement business and her hand fell away as he gave her a quick kiss on her cheek and left. There were screens partly round her and Kyle looked at them impatiently, hearing the quiet murmur of the hospital ward around them.

'I'm having you moved to a private room,' he said tightly. 'They're starting the procedure now.'

'There's no need...' she began, but he sat by the bed abruptly and ignored her.

'There's every need. I can't have you here in an open ward where anyone could come in and pester you. You'll be moved straight away, before I leave.'

'I—I don't even know where I am,' she murmured anxiously and he looked at her steadily, his eyes probing her face for some sign she couldn't fathom.

'A small hospital just outside London. If you had been seriously injured you would have been in the city by now but you're all right. Slight concussion and a bit of neck-whip.' He looked grim. 'You didn't even have a handbag with you, just a set of keys which I presume are for your own house. You had nothing more with you. They didn't even know your name.' He looked at her steadily. 'I assume you were leaving—escaping. Do you normally travel so light?'

He sounded angrily sarcastic and she closed her eyes again, making a very rapid escape from the cool grey glitter of his.

'I was going home to—to think.' She took a deep, shuddering breath. 'How did you find me if nobody knew——?'

'You gave them a clue. You kept repeating a name.'

She opened her eyes and looked at him, painfully puzzled, her brow furrowed with a growing pain and her mind not quite grasping his meaning. 'A name?'

'My name. You lay there saying "Kyle", until an intelligent nurse recognised you from your photograph in the paper. They got in touch with me. They were about one second ahead of the police, who used more scientific methods, like car registration, computers and a bit of gossip.'

She flushed, a wave of unexpected colour against her pale cheeks. 'I don't remember saying——'

'Don't let it worry you,' he murmured. 'I'm sure if you'd been in possession of your faculties you would have said Steven, or even Eliot.'

He stood abruptly as a nurse came in, followed very rapidly by a sister.

'She should rest now, Mr Maddison,' the sister said with a look that was part authority and part fascination. 'We'll get her moved and then you can see her later today.'

Kyle nodded briefly. 'I'll wait until you've moved her and then leave. Her brother will also want to see that she is more comfortable.'

Alexandra was embarrassed. She was quite comfortable apart from a growing headache and a stiff neck that defied any sort of movement. 'I—I can't move my head...' she began, and Kyle's eyes went to the sister, a quite alarming frown on his face.

'It's only stiff muscles,' she soothed, glancing anxiously at Kyle. 'She's been X-rayed. She's perfectly fine. This sort of accident is quite common.'

Kyle stayed away as Alexandra was wheeled to a lift and taken to another room on the next floor, a room that looked like the best room in a small hotel. The sister's anxiety gave way to bursts of conversation.

'We had no idea who you were, Miss Kent. Of course it's quite natural that Mr Maddison would want you in a nice, quiet room. I mean, he wouldn't want you to be in an ordinary ward, and then there's the visiting and...'

Alexandra was quite fascinated to realise that this rather starchy sister was just that bit scared of Kyle and she had probably never even seen him before. It wasn't really surprising. His power overwhelmed everyone, not least herself.

He was there as she was finally settled into bed. 'We'll get her own night attire here,' he said quietly, his eyes coolly looking over her white hospital gown. 'She seems to be in pain. I assume you're going to deal with that at once?'

He was assured that they were and Alexandra just lay there looking at him, greatly relieved that the sister was still there, hovering about as Kyle came over to the bed.

'I'll see you this evening,' he said quietly, looking down at her. 'We'll have all your things brought in within the hour.'

She didn't say there was no need to hurry. He would not have listened anyway. Her eyes closed before the brilliant, blazing grey of his gaze and she suddenly felt his lips on hers, a kiss so gentle that she could hardly believe it. Of course, Sister was there, her face flustered and pink as Kyle walked to the door and left. It had to be that. Kyle was quite capable of keeping up appearances indefinitely.

Steven came with her things; nightwear and her dressing-gown, toiletries and cosmetics and clothes for when she was ready to leave. 'Kyle sorted them out,' he confessed as she looked at him in some surprise. 'I didn't know what to get but he just went through your things and had them ready in no time.'

She didn't like the idea of anyone going through her things, let alone Kyle, and her face flushed as she noticed the silky undies ready for when she left hospital.

'You should have seen his face when we heard about the accident,' Steven said in some awe. 'That guy really loves you, Alex. He was—distraught.' He let the word run around his tongue, feeling quite pleased with it. 'Yes, that's what he was. I thought at one time he didn't much care.' He shot her a long look. 'I couldn't reckon it up, having met him. He's so tough. But I can see that it's just his way. He was...'

'Distraught?' Alexandra managed wryly. She couldn't envisage Kyle being distraught. Furious, yes. Distraught, never! He had probably been enraged that she had left without his permission and had got herself into a scrape that would reflect badly on him—driving a small, inexpensive car too.

'He says you're not to drive that car again,' Steven chipped in. 'He won't even have it repaired. He'll have a new one for you before you get out of here. Boy, what a brother-in-law he's going to make!'

'Steven,' Alexandra said cautiously, her eyes on his glowing face. 'I—I really think you should go—warily, with Kyle.'

There was a good deal of hero-worship on Steven's face at the moment, and she felt her heart sink as she faced the thought of his disappointment and disillusionment when this was all over and they were back to their own little house, Kyle out of their lives.

'Oh, I know he's a hard customer,' Steven said seriously. 'He sometimes looks really dangerous—when he's annoyed. I'm always a bit wary about that. I'll not overstep the mark even when he *is* my brother-in-law.'

That wasn't what she had meant at all, but she could hardly tell Steven that this delicious state of affairs was not to be.

'You look tired,' he said as her face became a little gloomy, her thoughts dark. 'I'll have to go. Kyle dropped me off and he'll be picking me up soon. If I tire you, he'll be after me like a shot. I've learned to watch my step. He's great when he knows I'm behaving myself.'

So Steven knew he hadn't been behaving himself before? It was one step closer to a cure, all of it due to Kyle. Her heart gave a little flutter. Maybe Kyle would call in and see her? When Steven had gòne she lay there watching the door, hoping he would come, but he didn't. Instead a nurse came in about half an hour later, her small frame hidden behind a huge basket of roses. They were beautiful, deep red and shockingly expensive-looking. No doubt he'd made a florist open up on a Sunday.

'From your fiancé,' the little nurse said with a smile. 'It's so romantic about you and Mr Maddison. I saw your picture in the papers. He's such a strong-looking man, so handsome. You looked like a fairy princess at the side of him at that smart place.' Her face went quite red and she put the roses down. 'Shall I give you the card?'

'Oh, yes, please.' She might as well play this through to the end. Kyle was obviously doing just that.

It was a tiny envelope from the florist's and it had just one thing on it: 'Kyle'. She slid it back into the envelope and put it on her table.

'I expect it's secret?' The romantically minded little nurse beamed and Alexandra smiled weakly, glad when she left. No, it wasn't a secret, only between Kyle and herself. If it had been an open card no doubt he would have written something more flowery. Why should he make the effort when only she would see it? They knew where they stood with each other, after all.

He came in the early evening, taking her completely by surprise. She hadn't been expecting anyone and she was lying with her eyes closed, not even bothering to look up when the door opened. She thought it was the nurse again—she had been 'seen to' until she felt like screaming. He just came and sat by the bed and she knew then. She could feel his presence, smell that faint tang of aftershave, feel his power.

She opened her eyes and he was looking straight at her, his expression peculiar. 'Did I wake you?'

She noticed again how deep and dark his voice was, how beautiful, and she just shook her head without thinking, the pain taking her by surprise as she moved her neck.

'You're still in pain?' He took her hand, his fingers warm and gentle, and tears stung at the back of her eyes. She needed Kyle. She had never needed anyone in her life as she needed him.

'It's only my neck,' she managed chokingly. 'They say it's going to be a lot better tomorrow. Thank you for the flowers. They—they impressed the nurse.'

'But not you.'

'They're beautiful, nice to look at.'

He let her hand go and leaned back, watching her, and she knew he had something to tell her. It filled her with panic. Could it be that he was sorry now that she had had an accident and was going to release her from this pact, to let her go free? It was what she had wanted but now she prayed silently that he would not do it. She wanted to stay with Kyle as long as she could, in any capacity.

'I want to talk about Steven,' he said seriously. 'Maybe I should leave it until you're feeling better but as you're lying here, no doubt thinking deep thoughts, it might be an idea to tell you my plans.'

'What plans?' she asked a little anxiously, worried that he seemed to be following her line of thinking.

'He should try to get into college at the end of the year,' he surprised her by saying. 'He's got a lot of talent. He's not just some mechanical amateur, he really understands machinery and he should have some qualifications.'

She just lay there looking at him, saying nothing, utterly surprised, and he looked at her wryly.

'Well, I've got this far without any remonstrations so I'll continue. I've mentioned it to him and he seems keen to go ahead. He'll be eighteen in a few months' time and he could go to college and get some sort of engineering degree. He did well at school, I hear.'

He did, before he took up with dubious companions.

'Could he get into college?' Alexandra asked worriedly. 'He's picked up a good deal of trouble recently.'

'I'll get him in,' Kyle said with that finality about his voice that told her he would have no difficulty at all.

'But when he applies for a grant they'll find out that——'

'He doesn't need a grant. I'll take care of all that sort of thing.'

'No!' She struggled to sit up, her face flushed with pain and embarrassment. 'You're nothing to do with us. We won't be any further in your debt.'

He looked at her quizzically. 'Nothing to do with you? I'm engaged to you, Alexandra. Surely Steven's future brother-in-law can pay for his further education?'

'You're *not* his future brother-in-law!' Alexandra said bitterly, sinking back to the pillows as the pain grew wildly. 'It's all so many lies, but the lies are for other people, not for you and me. We're nothing to each other at all.'

'That's hardly the truth either,' he said sardonically, moving to make the pillows comfortable, leaning over her and treating her very carefully. 'We *are* something to each other. We want each other. Today I nearly lost you, Alexandra, and I don't let anything slip through my fingers. I have every intention of marrying you if that's the only way I can get you.'

She just stared at him, her face almost whiter than the pillows, and he grimaced ruefully.

'Maybe I should have left this discussion until later but I never let things simply wait. That way they disappear, and I've no intention of letting you disappear.' He leaned further over her, a sort of smile on his face. He never expected any opposition, he had said he allowed none. She tried to shrink away but he cupped her face carefully with one long-fingered, powerful hand.

'Go to sleep, Alex,' he said softly, 'and don't have any nightmares. I've told you that I'll make you happy. I have every intention of doing so. You'll be treated like a queen, although at the moment you look more like a lost waif.'

His lips moved over hers, gently and carefully, suddenly deepening and then withdrawing, and she was still staring at him with dark, shocked eyes as he left.

He assumed that it was all arranged, that he only had to decide something and it would come to pass. Her head was too painful to think straight but there was a cold feeling inside. He was now ruthlessly intent on marrying her because he wanted her and for no other reason. It seemed that it was quite enough reason for him. She had no doubt whatever that she would be drenched in diamonds and furs, looked after like a prized possession while ever it lasted, and then what? He would move on, conquering fresh fields, wanting other women. And there was Dulcie Hepwarth and their 'special arrangement'.

She began to cry softly but it hurt her head, and when Sister came in she was quite shocked.

'Now then, Miss Kent,' she said briskly. 'We can't have this. Mr Maddison will be here tomorrow, I've no doubt. He can't sit by your bed all night, you know. You need a lot of rest if you're to get back home.'

Home! She would never get back home again. She didn't even want to. She wanted to be with Kyle, but not on his cool, logical terms, taken over and absorbed into his life while he wanted her, one minute after the next however long it lasted. He might think that was life, but she didn't.

She made no protest when the sister gave her a pain-killing injection. It was the only way she was going to sleep anyway.

Eliot came the next afternoon and she was so glad to see him that her face lit up. Sanity! He had brought a big bunch of flowers and they were ordinary, plain, just a big bunch like everyone else expected. His card was also ordinary. It said, 'Get well soon, love, from Eliot.'

He sat by the bed and chatted and a little colour came back into her face as she heard the latest gossip from work. So much happened in a single day with Kyle around, and apparently Janey had been given a talking-to from Kyle because of her 'preening' ways. Eliot made her laugh and she was still smiling as he stood to go.

'I'd better get back before somebody tells the boss I've had two hours for lunch.' He grinned. 'Get back to work, Alex. I know you're only shirking here.'

Her smile died as the door opened and Kyle stood there filling the doorway, his face thunderous. Eliot's smile died too. He always seemed to be caught out. It was a sort of destiny with Kyle around.

He left rapidly and Kyle advanced towards her bed with a menacing look that she had to fight hard to face. 'So it's still going on?' he bit out, his face hard and tight. 'It never stopped after all. He even takes time off work to sneak in here to see you!'

'He wasn't sneaking anywhere,' Alexandra protested. 'In any case, it's his own lunchtime.'

'At two-thirty?' he snapped sarcastically. 'That sort of lunchtime is for the higher echelons. Davis is not in that bracket.'

His eyes fell on the bunch of flowers still on Alexandra's bed and her hand came out to clutch them as she thought he was about to throw them to the floor. He was only interested in the card.

'"Get well soon, love,"' he read out in a corrosive voice. 'And it's not still going on? I broke up a really hot romance, didn't I?'

'You just don't understand,' Alexandra said wearily. 'People like you just don't understand ordinary mortals. He's my friend, that's all, and if you punish him——'

'I wouldn't punish your friend, Alexandra,' he rasped. 'I suppose you think you need a friend with me around.' He glared at the inoffensive flowers she was clutching protectively. 'You can let them go. I'm not about to tear the petals off.'

He turned away, pacing about angrily, his hands in his pockets, and then stood to look out of the window. 'I suppose I've upset you again?' he queried more quietly. 'You're perfectly safe and so is Davis. When you're well you can leave. There's no need to stay here hiding in bed, so don't let the thought grow.'

So he was letting her go—her days of being a prisoner were over. She was too stunned to cry and she would never have cried in any case, not while he was there. She could only see empty days without him and she kept a tight hold on herself.

She couldn't think of anything to say and he suddenly turned and left, not even looking back at her. It seemed to break a barrier that had held her fast. He hadn't even asked how she was, his cold anger such a contrast to Eliot's pleasant ways.

When the doctor came in half an hour later to see her she tackled him straight away. 'Am I perfectly all right, doctor?' she asked straightforwardly. 'Apart from a headache and a neck that's stiff, do I have anything wrong with me at all?'

'Nothing whatever, Miss Kent.' He smiled, not knowing what was on her mind, his manner soothing and reassuring.

'Then I could leave now?' she asked, quite shocking him.

'Theoretically, providing you were going straight to bed for a couple of days. Mr Maddison, however——'

'If Mr Maddison didn't exist you'd allow me to go home and go to bed there?' she asked calmly.

'Well, yes.'

'Then that's precisely what I intend to do. If you could arrange it, Sister?' she finished with a very determined look at the sister's flushed face.

There was nothing they could do, and an hour later Alexandra stood by her bed, dressed and ready to leave. She was not as strong as she had thought and her legs had a tendency to give way, but she had phoned a taxi, using the telephone by her bed for the first time ever and charging the trip to Kyle. They did not demur and

she was not one bit repentant. Kyle had got her into this
mess—he could pay for getting her out.

'What about your beautiful flowers?' the little nurse
asked, and Alexandra looked at the roses, her eyes trying
not to see Kyle's face as he had meticulously bought the
right thing.

'Put them on the ward,' she suggested. 'They'll cheer
somebody up.' She clutched Eliot's flowers. 'I'm taking
these with me.'

She still had her house keys. They were in the pocket
of her jeans and she gave her own home address when
the taxi came, sinking back into the seat and wishing
she was already in bed.

The house was so empty, as if nobody had ever lived
there at all, and to her relief Mrs Nash was nowhere to
be seen. She put the kettle on and then wearily went to
change into her nightdress. She would have to go to bed,
she knew that, but here she would be quite alone and
she would not open the door if Kyle came. Not that he
would. Hadn't he told her she could go?

With her dressing-gown on she sank to the settee, realising she had not even enough energy to make herself
a drink, and her eyes closed, the effort of getting up and
making the journey catching up with her fast.

She heard keys in the door and Kyle came striding in
before she could move, his face forbidding as he saw
her half lying on the settee.

'How—how——?'

'Steven's keys,' he said, tossing them in his hand and
then putting them in his pocket. He looked at her
severely. 'You do the strangest things, Miss Kent. I find
myself quite puzzled by your behaviour.'

'You said I could go,' she reminded him wearily. 'You
said I could go—and I went.'

'I said you could go when you were well enough,' he
corrected. 'You are not well enough, and in any case I

did not say that you could leave me. You and I have some unfinished business.'

'I've come home,' she argued weakly, and he came across and simply scooped her up into his arms.

'No, pansy-eyes. You've left home. Home is where I am and leaving home is not allowed. Come along.'

He held her carefully and made for the door and she began to protest, her hand plucking at his sleeve.

'I can't! I'm not dressed!'

'You're quite respectable. I won't expect you to board a bus in your nightie. My car is outside.'

'The neighbours——'

'Are watching with interest. Anything else?' He opened the front door and looked down at her, his lips quirking, and for once there was only amusement, no derision.

'I have to look at the kettle,' she said, giving up the fight.

'There now,' he soothed mockingly. 'I'll see that you have a kettle to look at as soon as we get back. You can borrow one from Graves. I promised you happiness. If you crave kettles you shall have one.'

'I have to pull the plug out. Please don't make fun of me, Kyle.'

'You would rather have a shaking? The tendency is there. While you talk like a small lunatic I'm able to suppress my desire to beat you. As to the kettle, it will cope very nicely. You shall have a better one.'

He walked out to his car and gently put her inside, ignoring the twitching curtains and the fact that Mrs Nash was now firmly at her door, expecting explanations. He got into the car and then waved cheerfully at them as he drove off.

Alexandra sank back against the seat, closing her eyes. She was captured again and she felt ridiculously weepy, but she also knew she was going home. Kyle was right. It was home wherever he was.

'How did you know I'd left?' she asked in a choked little voice.

'I went back as soon as my temper had subsided. The bird had flown and Sister was outraged. A nurse was just putting your flowers on the big ward,' he added quietly.

It reminded her that Eliot's were still in the living-room, out of water. 'Oh, I left Eliot's flowers to die,' she said sadly.

'So I noticed,' he murmured with satisfaction.

'He cares about me,' she protested, and he glanced across at her pale face.

'So do I, Alex. I care enough about you to want you and to fight to get you. If the positions had been reversed I would not have walked meekly out of that room after seeing you looking so ill. I would have picked you up and taken you home with me, which is precisely what I'm doing now.'

What was the use of arguing with him? She just didn't feel up to it any more. She lay back and closed her eyes again and he stopped, lowered her seat back and wrapped a car rug round her before driving carefully off again. Tears stung at her eyes. She was to be cosseted, cared for like a treasure while his interest lasted. He had dealt viciously with everyone who had tried to hurt her and it was only Eliot's ability to sink into the background that had saved him.

It wasn't what she wanted. She sighed as contrary thoughts flooded into her mind. Why did she feel so safe again? She wasn't safe. She had never been so unsafe in her whole life. But she was conscious of Kyle beside her, of his capable, powerful hands on the wheel, of that strong, handsome face and those grey, intelligent eyes.

He started to laugh, the soft, dark sound startling her, and she opened her eyes to see his face quietly amused.

He glanced across at her, laughter in his eyes, a thing she hardly ever saw.

'I'm just wondering how many more times you're going to need rescuing,' he volunteered when she just looked at him in astonishment. 'At this rate I'm going to get nothing done at all. The business affairs of the Maddison Group are running themselves today.' His eyes went back to the road. 'Rest quietly,' he ordered softly. 'I'll have you home and safely tucked up in bed before you know it. Graves can bring you a selection of kettles to choose from.'

He sat there smiling to himself and she closed her eyes obediently, her heart pounding away. Did he seem more gentle, softer? Maybe it was because she was so obviously ill, or maybe it was because once again he had won? She was too weary to pursue the thoughts and she fell asleep in the warmth and comfort of the car.

Kyle moved the car rug aside, picked her up and carried her into the house, where both Steven and Graves were waiting in the hall.

'Alex! I don't know what's come over you!' Steven began as soon as he saw that she was safe and being handled carefully. 'You used to be the most sensible person.'

Long, long ago before I met Kyle, Alexandra thought. She was too weary to answer, too weary to lift her head from Kyle's shoulder, and he made straight for the stairs.

'I'll get her into bed and then you can bring some tea to her room, Graves,' he said briskly.

Her room! She had a room at home, her own home, but Kyle wouldn't let her go. 'Don't go on about the kettle, Kyle,' she murmured plaintively, her eyes closed.

'Would I do such a thing?' he mocked softly. Inside her room he slid her to her feet by the bed and then removed her dressing-gown.

'Kyle!' Her small protest and flushed face seemed to amuse him all over again.

'I've seen plenty of ladies in their nightwear,' he taunted.

'I don't doubt it.' Her eyes flashed angrily in spite of her aches and her utter weariness, and he swung her into his arms, putting her into bed and pulling the sheets over her.

'Just say the word and it's only you,' he said huskily as he arranged the pillows comfortably.

'Until it's over.' She turned her head and closed her eyes, shocked that she was even contemplating such a thing.

'Perhaps it will never be over,' he said softly. 'Perhaps we'll just go on being wild about each other forever.'

She couldn't answer. It was so impossible, not in Kyle's character. Even Dulcie Hepwarth knew that, whatever she was to him. She kept her eyes closed until he had gone.

Graves fussed over her. A few weeks ago she would never have believed it but he came with tea, poured it and hovered around until she sank back to the pillows.

'Thank you, Graves.' She opened her eyes and watched him walk to the door, his step very dignified. 'Do I have to call you Graves?' she suddenly said. 'It's not a bit friendly.'

'It's expected Miss Alexandra, and I'm used to it. In any case, my first name is Sidney. It's not a name I'm at all fond of.'

No, he wouldn't be, she could see that. It didn't fit him at all. As he closed the door she suddenly realised he had called her Miss Alexandra, not Miss Kent. Even Graves had decided that she was 'part of the family'. She made a little fretful sound as she turned on her side, and when Steven and Kyle came up later to see her she was fast asleep. Steven looked greatly pleased to see her safely in bed. He just couldn't understand the scrapes she was getting into lately. He tiptoed out and went back to the garage but Kyle lingered, watching her.

Even when she was asleep and hurt, her face pale and bruised, he wanted her. He felt uncomfortably aroused, his imagination seeing her in his own bed. His determination frightened her, he knew that, but without it he would never own her. In any case, he was himself, all he could be. He closed the door and walked away, his face taut and an angry light in his eyes.

CHAPTER NINE

THE pain in her neck woke Alexandra in the night and she struggled out of bed to the bathroom for aspirin, the bright lights making matters worse when she switched them on. Everything was hard to find, her mind seeing not this bathroom but her own at home, and she knocked several things out of the cabinet before her hand closed on the thing she was looking for.

'What are you doing?'

Kyle's dark voice made her jump and she dropped the small glass bottle, the contents spilling over the floor, seemingly a million tiny white tablets.

'Look what you've made me do,' she complained tearfully, her hand clutching her neck. 'I'll have to bend right down there to get some.'

He simply picked her up, making straight for the bed in spite of her tearful protests.

'What are you doing in here?' Alexandra asked fretfully. 'How did you know that——?'

'You're a remarkably noisy person,' he mocked softly, 'I'm surprised that everyone else is sleeping. In any case, I was listening for you. I've got something better than aspirin. When I went to the hospital the doctor gave me some tablets. He was outraged at your behaviour but he knew you'd have trouble. Stay there and I'll get them.'

Alexandra sat on the edge of the bed holding her head; it felt as if it might drop off, and it was throbbing painfully, her neck muscles sore and tight. She had wanted to cling to Kyle when he had lifted her, it had seemed so right. When he came back in she squinted up at him—

it was all she could manage. 'You're not undressed,' she said foolishly, and he smiled down at her mockingly.

'Sorry to disappoint you. I was reading.'

'It's two o'clock. You'll be tired tomorrow.'

'Alex! No mothering.' His teasing smile died quickly and she felt very tearful.

'I wasn't. I was just thinking how you'd feel tomorrow at work and——'

'Take your tablets,' he said firmly, holding a glass of water and handing her two large white tablets.

She swallowed them with difficulty and still sat there until he lifted her into bed. But she didn't want him to leave her, her arms winding around his neck without thought, and he held her tightly for a second.

'I wasn't . . . I was just worried about how you'd feel and——'

'Don't, Alex,' he said tightly as she looked at him with pained, dark eyes, her arms still clinging. 'You're ill and in pain and I know it. This is neither the time nor the place.'

She still coiled against him though and he looked down at her trembling lips, his mouth tight, but a sensuous flare of desire streaking through him that was utterly beyond his control.

'Close your eyes,' he ordered in a taut voice, but she still looked at him, her face pale and dazed, her dark eyes spellbound.

'If I do, you'll go away.'

'Alex,' he groaned, coming down with her as he lowered her to the pillows, her clinging arms refusing to release him, 'why now, when I've been going mad to have you for weeks?'

She was sure he hadn't but she couldn't remember; he was close and she softened to him, a small smile growing on her lips. It was echoed in his eyes and his arms gathered her close carefully, surrendering to the urge to be near her.

'You do quite crazy things, Miss Kent, and this is one of them. You know perfectly well that I don't want to go away.' His lips brushed her cheeks lightly, his breathing suddenly uneven, and his arms tensed when she murmured contentedly.

'You walk into danger,' he whispered thickly. 'You're in danger now.'

'Are you angry?' She looked up into his face, her soft dark eyes calling like a siren, and his face grew strained with desire, his eyelids heavy.

'No. Desperate!'

His lips trailed over hers, tasting her, revelling in her sweetness, his fingers flexing against the soft warmth of her. Pleasure flooded through her, drowning out pain, and she moaned, her lips parting invitingly, and Kyle gasped, his mouth opening over hers. His body responded with a will of its own, overcoming his common sense, his knee moving possessively to part her thighs, his hands coming to cup her face.

It hurt, all her face hurt and she winced, making him look up at her quickly and move away as he saw the pain in her eyes.

'I don't know why you're so determined to mother me, or Steven for that matter,' he said ruefully as he covered her with the sheets and stood up, his eyes moving over her disappointed face. 'You can't even take care of yourself.'

'I can. I——'

'No, you can't, Alex. You just invited the very thing you fight to avoid and you're not even well enough to stand by yourself. When you come to me it's going to last all night and you're going to be in full possession of your senses. I want every part of you but I want it given freely.'

'I feel dizzy,' she complained pitifully and he suddenly grinned, the fierce sexual tension draining away.

'It's the tablets. They're strong pain-killers. The doctor thought you'd need them. Now *there's* a man who knows what he's doing, which is more than I do right now.' He bent forward and lowered his mouth to hers, unable to resist the trembling sweetness.

'I don't want to go to sleep,' she murmured fretfully, knowing perfectly well somewhere inside that she was behaving very badly, quite out of character.

'Don't worry,' he whispered against her lips. 'You'll soon be sleeping with me—very soon, Alex.'

She must have been asleep even before he left because she couldn't remember him going, but a smile was edging her lips and she never saw the bright triumph in his grey eyes that momentarily masked the raw hunger.

In the morning he was gone before she was even awake, and when Graves brought her breakfast she said very clearly that she would be up for lunch. He stood and looked at her determinedly.

'Now then, Miss Alexandra. Mr Maddison knew that was just what you'd do and he left me strict orders. You're not to move from this bed.'

She was feeling a lot better and smiled up at him mischievously. 'How do you propose to stop me?'

His face reddened but he looked at her very firmly. 'I'm to ring Mr Maddison at once and I shall do so.'

'Oh, I'm sorry, Graves,' Alexandra said contritely. 'I feel so much better that I wanted to joke. I'll stay here, don't worry.'

'That's all right, miss,' he said, looking relieved, a small smile growing. 'I knew you'd be sensible. I do have a daughter not much older than you, though,' he added as a soft threat as he left, and Alexandra burst into laughter. Kyle certainly chose the men he had around him with great care.

The thought of Kyle brought a flush to her own face as she began to remember how she had behaved last night, but she still felt the excitement of it even though it had been sheer madness. Being hurt, escaping from him and being brought firmly back seemed to have changed things, although she wasn't sure quite how. She felt differently inside.

He had said he cared enough about her to want her and to have picked her up and taken her home with him when she had been looking so hurt and ill. She began to dream of him being in the same place as Eliot, facing an angry man who was prepared for trouble. Kyle would have ignored it and snatched her up.

She snatched her thoughts up at that. What was wrong with her? She was glorying in being captured, quite forgetting how this whole thing had started. It would be as well to remember that Kyle went to Dulcie Hepwarth when he wanted to. Rules were for other people.

She was very glad when Steven wandered in, his face lighting up when he saw her looking so much better. 'Kyle wants me to go to college,' he announced in his usual way, straight out and no preamble. He sat on the edge of the bed and poured himself some of her tea, his eyes laughing. 'I didn't get a silver pot with *my* breakfast. What do you think of the idea—college, I mean?'

'What do you think?' she asked carefully. It almost made her hold her breath to see the difference in him. Kyle had changed him and the shock of her accident had done the rest, apparently.

'You're hedging, Sis. Normally you're not long in giving opinions, or orders.'

'You'll be the one to go, not me,' she said quickly. Did she give orders and opinions so often? Had she been smothering Steven?

'I'm dead keen to go,' he admitted, giving her a sidelong glance that used to horrify her but now merely intrigued her, and she realised it was because Kyle now had the responsibility. She seemed to have handed both her life and her responsibilities over to Kyle.

'Then go. Agree to it,' she urged. 'It will open up a new world for you, Steven.'

'Kyle's got an engineering firm in Canada. Did you know that?'

Alexandra shook her head. No, she didn't know that. She hadn't bothered to get to know him at all. It had been one long fight. All she knew was what Ian Jagger had told her. 'He's suggesting you go there?'

'For a spell after college, if I do OK. It would be exciting, a chance to see something of the world.'

It would. She looked at him seriously, her head on one side, and nodded. 'Start planning, then.'

'Oh, we have! Last night after dinner when you were asleep, Kyle and I were going through a few college possibilities.' He suddenly stopped and looked at her closely. 'You don't mind? Kyle said not to tell you until——'

'I don't mind a bit.' She smiled. She didn't—she felt safe and comfortable, hardly any pain left, except a queer little pain inside when she thought of Kyle in the office and imagined those strong hands that had held her last night and had wanted to hold her closer still

Five days later Alexandra was up and about, almost completely recovered, much to the relief of Graves, who had faced imagined mutiny every day although she had behaved very well indeed. She had seen almost nothing of Kyle except for a brief moment each evening when he'd come home and called in to enquire how she had been. She'd supposed he had been working with his usual driving energy at the office and had little time left when he'd come home, but she had missed him badly and he had seemed to be keeping very well clear of her. She'd known he had been out almost every night, too, and that had meant only one thing—Dulcie.

It changed her attitude. Her behaviour when she had been ill and they way she had been when he'd come to help her now embarrassed her, making her shy and uneasy when he was there. She suffered great pangs of jealousy too. It made her avoid his eyes, and when she was at last given leave to eat her dinner downstairs with Steven she was tremblingly anxious to find Kyle there.

His face was utterly bland and composed, his manner merely quietly solicitous, and she found herself muttering when he spoke to her. It began to embarrass her even more and when Steven left to go to his room she got up hastily.

'No coffee?' Kyle asked quietly and she shook her head.

'No, thank you. It might give me a headache.'

'Perhaps you're afraid that I will?' There was anger in his voice and she just fled.

He walked into her room almost behind her, giving her no time to compose her feelings. He attacked straight away, a very normal thing for Kyle. 'So we're back where we started?' he grated. 'The clinging, willing Miss Kent is not with us any more?'

'I'm sure you've had plenty of clinging each night since,' she blazed, jealousy ripping through her.

'You're jealous,' he said slowly, his eyes flaring with triumph. 'You're jealous of Dulcie.'

Alexandra turned her back on him quickly, her flush fading to pallor, and she heard him move, her skin tingling as he came to stand behind her. His hands came to her waist, tightening, his fingers spreading out over her stomach.

'If you want me here each night then marry me, Alex,' he said seductively. 'I want you. Marry me and there'll be nobody else.'

'You don't need to marry me,' Alexandra managed shakily. 'You've got everything you set out to get—all we have to do is live out this time for Steven.'

'I haven't got everything I set out to get. I want *you*.' His mouth moved over her bare shoulder, his lips parted, his breath warm, sending flutters of excitement over her body. 'I'll have to marry one day and right now I can't think of any woman I'm going to want as much as I want you.'

'I can't! It's madness! I don't want——!'

He spun her round, his arm tightly around her, his hand tilting her face to his, his mouth over hers. 'Marry me. Marry me. Marry me,' he murmured over and over until his lips closed over her own, possessive, demanding and thrilling, and her whole world dissolved into flame.

He had never kissed her like this before, as if he already owned her, and her legs turned to water as she melted against him, unable to resist. His hand came to her breast, teasing and arousing, and her moans mingled with his as he lifted her, his lips never leaving hers as he placed her on the bed.

'Now, Alex, now,' he groaned. 'This time I don't want you to close your eyes. I want your arms round me, those trembling lips telling me to stay.'

She coiled her slender arms around his neck and he moved completely over her, his body aroused and impatient, his lips seeking hers hotly as she softened beneath him. His fingers were impatient too on the zip of her dress, and she heard the delicate fabric rip as he moved it from her and tossed it aside, his mouth closing over her breast instantly.

Pain seared through her at the insistent pull of his lips. It was a feeling mixed with rapture but she gasped his name and he looked up at her, his eyes dark and demanding.

'I'm frightening you?' he asked thickly, his hand moulding her breast. 'Don't you want me, Alex?' There was naked desire on his face, almost a wild look, and it hypnotised her.

'Yes, oh, yes!'

His hand cupped her head, lifting her face to his, his other hand arching her against him until she could feel the feverish heat of his body, the taut power of his desire. 'Then tell me you'll marry me, Alex! Tell me or I'll take you now. Lord knows, I want to!' he said hoarsely.

'I'll marry you.'

It was madness, crazy, but she never wanted him to go, never wanted to be out of those strong, demanding arms. It did not make him gentle. His whole body seemed to burn with triumph.

'This weekend.'

'But——' He cut off her gasp of protest with burning lips, kissing her until she could say nothing at all.

'I've got a licence,' he said thickly when he let her mouth escape from his, his breathing uneven. 'I've had it for ages.'

'You didn't know that I'd——'

'I knew,' he said tautly. 'I never intended letting you go.'

Other words he had said came swimming into her mind... 'I have to have those shares. Therefore, your aunt will sell.' Aunt Cora had sold. Kyle didn't just do things, he planned things. He had told her himself. Cold fingers touched her heart, bringing her back to reality. She had no illusions whatever about Kyle. The women in his life were no secret. She was letting herself be engulfed by his desire and her own.

Alexandra stiffened, but before she could speak there was a soft tapping on the door and she heard Steven's voice.

'Alex? Can I come in?'

'No!' Kyle answered before she could even think of answering and she heard Steven's embarrassed apology, her own face flooding with colour.

'What will he think?' she asked in horror as Kyle slowly stood and looked down at her.

'He'll think twice about knocking on your door again,' he said sardonically, his eyes moving over her as she lay looking up at him.

'It may have been important,' she retorted. His face darkened and he lifted her up, straightening her slip before pulling her into his arms.

'Then he'll solve it himself, or tell me,' he assured her grimly. 'There's nobody at all to mother now, Alexandra. Steven grew up while you weren't looking and, in any case, you belong to me.'

'I don't. I——'

'You will after this weekend,' he murmured as his lips closed over hers hard and fast.

'And what about Dulcie? What about——?'

'I told you that after we're married there'll only be you,' he said harshly. He turned and walked out, leaving her looking at the closed door. Then what? How long would it last? Her mind battled between common sense and her desire to be with Kyle, but deep inside she already knew that her love would win.

She didn't know how she would face Steven next morning but he just grinned at her, not one bit embarrassed.

'Sorry about the interruption last night,' he said with a laugh. 'For a moment there I forgot you were engaged.'

'Did—did you want something important?' she asked, realising that the embarrassment was all hers.

'Not really. I figured it out for myself.' He gave her a little peck on the cheek and disappeared, the Bugatti beckoning, and Alexandra sat down to her breakfast in splendid isolation, noting with no real surprise that the silver teapot appeared when it was her breakfast in question. Graves too had decided she was to be treated like a queen, and Steven had grown up. Kyle was right— he was always right. She thought about the weekend and her hands trembled. She didn't know Kyle. It would be just like taking a lover. She blushed hotly and Graves hovered over her.

'Are you all right, Miss Alexandra? No headaches?'

'No, I'm quite all right, thank you,' she managed, sinking back in her chair as he smiled and left with his usual dignified step.

All right? She was mad. She had to be! But she thought about Kyle and her cheeks flushed again. Maybe he was right, maybe it would last forever. She knew it would with her because she loved him as madly as he wanted her.

Kyle came home early, driving up to the house almost immediately after lunch, but he didn't come in and Alexandra walked to the window, intrigued to see Kyle and Steven in deep conversation before they disappeared into the garage.

Minutes later she heard the sound of an engine and her own eyes began to smile as she realised what it was. Steven had turned his magic touch on the Bugatti.

She ran outside and was on the steps as Kyle drove it out, Steven almost dancing along beside him, and then there was another long discussion before Kyle climbed out and handed the whole thing over to Steven.

He drove past Alexandra, waving and grinning, and Kyle walked over to stand by her and watch as Steven and the splendid car disappeared down the drive.

'Is it finished?'

'Not yet, but it's mobile. That brother of yours is a very fast learner.'

She glanced up at him secretly, almost feasting her eyes on him, looking away quickly when he suddenly shot a glance at her and caught the expression on her face. 'Do—do you trust him?' she asked with shy huskiness.

'I do.' His face was thoughtful as he gazed down the drive. 'I trust him so much that if he let me down I think I'd kill him. He's become a necessary part of the establishment.' The Bugatti reappeared and Kyle suddenly grinned. 'I'll take you for a jolly spin, Lady Alexandra.'

She had never seen him so light-hearted and, as Steven stopped and got out, Kyle lifted her and swung her into the seat. He grinned at Steven, who assumed a definite nineteen-twenties look and shouted, 'Toodle-pip!'

Graves was there too, by Steven on the steps, and Alexandra knew that this was home. Nowhere else would ever be home again.

'Steven is—is fond of you,' she said shakily as they chugged down towards the gates, and to her dismay Kyle did not answer. He waited until they had made a turn ready to go back and then he pulled up, leaving the engine running.

'I know.' He stared straight ahead, the light-heartedness leaving him. 'Are you—fond of me?'

'I—I agreed to marry you,' Alexandra murmured, her face flushed. Fond of him? She adored him, hard and unfeeling though he was for most of the time.

'That's not what I asked!' He spun round to glare at her, his expression softening when he saw her face. 'Am I winning, Alex?' he asked quietly, turning her towards him.

'Don't you always?' She avoided looking at him and he bent his head, his lips brushing hers.

'I'm tired of keeping out of your way, woman,' he muttered thickly. 'I don't usually have to step carefully around anything I want.' His hands began to move over her, almost tentatively, and then he pulled her into his arms, his mouth capturing hers, kissing her searingly. He let her go when she was breathless and trembling. 'What you do to me is not too easy to take,' he told her huskily. 'I don't particularly like being ensnared.'

'You—you're not,' she managed tremblingly but he didn't answer, and before she had even begun to recover they were back, facing Steven's astonished looked.

'Don't tell me you were scared, Alex, at that speed!'

'No. She's tough,' Kyle rasped, marching off into the house. At the door he relented. 'I'll be back in a minute when I've changed. You've done a brilliant job on that car, Steven.'

Steven looked at Alex and shook his head in bewilderment. 'I thought he was annoyed and he's not at all. I wish I understood him like you do, Alex.'

She almost burst into tears. She didn't understand Kyle at all. The only thing she understood was that she loved him and that he wanted her almost wildly. When he came downstairs and ignored her, going off to spend the rest of the afternoon pottering about in the garage with Steven, she felt lonely and restless, even jealous of Steven. Kyle had turned everything upside-down.

At midnight she was still not asleep. She had spent so much time resting, taking no kind of physical exercise, and on top of that the aching need to be close to Kyle had made it impossible to sleep. She went down to make herself a drink, staying in the kitchen and simply walking in circles until she gave up the idea of sleep at all, collected a book and went back to the stairs.

Kyle appeared as she got to the top and he stood looking down at her as she hesitated. 'You're not a burglar, then?' he enquired softly. 'What's wrong? Were you intent on escape only to find that Graves locks up too thoroughly?'

'I wouldn't try to escape in my nightie and dressing-gown,' Alexandra muttered, looking hastily away from his eyes. He looked on edge, fierce and restless as if he had very little control of himself, and she remembered how he had always had tight control over everything, himself included. Was she doing this to him?

'You've travelled light before, if I recall.'

'I just couldn't sleep.'

'I'm not doing particularly well in that direction myself.' He stared at her silently and she slipped past him, making for her room. She dared not look at him. Everything inside her was quivering with need. She wanted his arms around her and his own desire was transmitting itself to her, making her tremble.

'Alex!' As she reached her door he was right there behind her, his hand on her arm as he turned her back towards him. 'Don't go, Alex,' he said thickly.

'I—I'll have to try and get some sleep.' She looked down, studying the carpet as if her life depended on it, her heart thudding like thunder.

'Sleep with me,' he begged huskily and she couldn't answer, the book almost falling from her suddenly limp hands, because she wanted to. She wanted to be close to Kyle and have a hold over him that nobody else had. She had fought against the engagement but now she was terrified that the marriage would not happen, that something would occur to put it off forever.

'Alex,' he murmured deeply, 'come with me. You're driving me mad.'

She just handed him the book and he put it down on the nearby table, standing terribly still until she looked up at him with soft dark eyes.

'Come to me, Alex,' he whispered, and she walked into his arms as he reached for her. His lips fused with hers, his arms lifting her with no pause at all, and she wound her arms around his neck, her ears telling her

that Kyle had closed her door and that he was taking
her with him, her mind hearing nothing but her own
heartbeats and the joy mixed with fear that asked her
why she was doing this.

In his room he kicked the door closed and then slid
her to her feet by the bed, his hands cupping her face
as he lifted it for his kisses. He said nothing at all even
when he undressed her and lay her on the bed; his eyes
burned her as he threw off his own clothes and then he
drew her close, his body on fire, his movements almost
feverish.

He was silent and passionate, his kisses and caresses
bringing moans from her lips until she threw back her
head and pleaded with him, 'Kyle! Say something to me.'
She didn't know what she wanted him to say, but his
ardour overwhelmed her even through the excitement
and she longed for soft words, gentleness.

'I can't,' he muttered thickly, his lips burning her skin.
'What do you want me to say? That I need you? I'm
proving that. I want to own you completely, trap you
beneath me and never let you go.' He looked up at her
with darkened grey eyes, his head raised from her breast.
'Do I frighten you, Alex? I can't promise not to hurt
you. All I can hope is that you want me enough
because——'

He looked desperate, as if even now she would spring
up and race to safety. Safety was not what she wanted
and she suddenly understood his lack of words. Love
blazed through her and she never let him finish his sentence—she pulled his head to hers and moved against
him softly.

She felt desire race across his skin and she gasped as
he suddenly possessed her, his mouth stifling her cry.
His heart threatened to leave his body, a groan torn from
his throat as he felt her tightly around him. She was
peace and pleasure, all woman, sweet-smelling and

silken. He had known he could never be gentle with her and she was so soft and slender but his passion soared out of control, a raw ache inside, and he took her with him racing to the clouds, staying there with her until he brought her back to earth, trembling and shaken in his arms, her face wet with salty tears.

When the raw, painful sound of his breathing had softened to normality he looked down at her, unable even now to leave her, and she opened tear-wet eyes to meet his brilliant grey gaze.

'Why, Alex?' he asked thickly. 'Are you crying because you regret the sacrifice or because I hurt you?'

She shook her head, unable to speak. It was no sacrifice. She had needed words of love but she had never expected those, and he had never promised any.

His hand stroked her face, almost tenderly, and he surprised her by kissing away the remaining tears. 'I always knew I would hurt you,' he murmured regretfully. 'It's the way you make me feel and I suppose it's the way I am.' His eyes darkened as his gaze raced over her, fastening on her trembling lips. 'You wanted me, though. Maybe now that I own you...'

His voice trailed away huskily and she felt desire shudder through him again as his lips claimed hers.

Next morning Kyle was gone and she opened her eyes slowly, aware of her surroundings immediately. She was lethargic, sweetly pained inside, and she was reluctant to leave Kyle's bed after a long night of his passion. She wished he had stayed. If just this once he had left the office to its own devices. She needed him with her today especially, but she resolutely went to her own room and prepared to face the day and face Kyle's questioning and penetrating gaze when he came home.

His eyes had been questioning more than once in the soft lamplight, but he had said nothing. There were not even passionate words from Kyle. His whole being seemed only intent on owning her. Words just never came, only whispers of yearning that she never even understood.

She was surprised to see Steven appear at breakfast all dressed up, wearing a suit. He looked at least twenty-one, a smart, handsome young man, no baby brother at all.

'This gear more to your taste?' he asked with a wide grin.

'Did Kyle...?'

'He supervised only,' Steven said loftily. 'He advised me to spend some of my money.' He shrugged, a habit he seemed to have picked up from Kyle. 'I don't mind Kyle telling me what to do. He's pretty clever.'

Diabolically clever, Alexandra corrected mentally, although colour flooded her face when his name was even mentioned.

'I'm going to London to meet him for lunch,' Steven continued. 'I'm going there and back by train. We're seeing a man about college, but Kyle's got a busy afternoon.' He glanced round as a car pulled up by the house. 'Here's my taxi. See you later.'

He was gone before she had really digested it all. A man about college? Kyle would be pulling another of those well-oiled strings. And he had been right—Steven had grown up when she hadn't been looking. She sat there cradling her cup in her hands, waiting for grief to hit her, but it never did. She was free of responsibility, free of worry. There was only Kyle. She belonged to him and this weekend she was going to marry him.

Suddenly she wanted to sing and dance for joy. She was warm and safe and Kyle wanted her enough to marry her. Love would come if she loved him enough—and she did. When his passion was not so wild, when he knew she would not leave, he would be tender, she was sure of that. He had promised her happiness.

She spent the morning just looking at her clothes, wondering what she should buy to get married in, wondering if they would go away for a few days, and after lunch she was still sitting at the table trying to make her mind up what to do about shopping when Graves came in and spoke quietly, his face anxious.

'Miss Alexandra, there's a visitor—it's Miss Hepwarth. Shall I show her into the drawing-room?'

'Does she want to see me?' Alexandra asked with an expression that matched his, her own anxiety mounting with frightening speed.

'She knows Mr Maddison is not here, Miss Alexandra,' he said grimly. 'I think she wants to see you.'

This was it, then, the confrontation, and Kyle nowhere near to protect her. What was she thinking of? She had never needed protecting. She stood and looked at Graves, seeing the annoyed sympathy in his eyes, and her hand went instinctively to his arm. 'Wheel her in,' she said firmly.

His step was more dignified than ever as he went to the hall, and Alexandra knew she had captured his affections without even trying. He seemed fond of Steven too and she felt that they both belonged here, part of the family, part of Kyle.

CHAPTER TEN

IN DAYLIGHT Dulcie Hepworth looked neither so glamorous nor so young. She drifted in, her feet hardly seeming to touch the floor, but it was all technique, all practised movement, and Alexandra found that she was not anxious any more.

'The rumour is out that Kyle intends to marry you,' Dulcie said as soon as she was seated. 'I came to warn you not to take that step.'

'That's very kind of you,' Alexandra said wryly, 'but Kyle and I have already decided. You're perfectly aware that we're engaged, and we're getting married this weekend.'

'Well, I've heard that one before,' Dulcie said with a smile. 'I suppose he's got a special licence and he can't wait for you any longer? My dear, haven't you found out yet how Kyle operates? He's a taker. You'll never make it to the altar but you'll certainly make it to his bedroom. I'm surprised you haven't made it that far yet, but you had an accident, didn't you? That may account for it.'

'How do you know I haven't——?' Alexandra began, but Dulcie's hand waved her remarks aside.

'He's bringing up the marrying bit. He never wastes his time on unnecessary things. You must be tougher than you look. They don't usually get this far.'

'I don't think you know anything about Kyle and me,' Alexandra said hotly, fighting down the doubts and clinging on to her dreams. 'You may have a special arrangement with Kyle——'

Dulcie's eyes blinked rapidly—apparently she was astonished that Kyle had told Alexandra that. 'Yes, we have a special arrangement,' she said quietly. 'I'm always there. You see, I understand him and I'll always be there. He'll never marry you, or me, or anyone else. Marriage to Kyle is unhappiness. His parents divorced and left him with an old man who was downright wicked——'

'I know about Kyle's grandfather,' Alexandra interrupted, blessing Ian and his gossip.

'But you didn't meet him. I did. Kyle and I were in America for one of my shows and the old man came down to see him. I heard the way he talked, the way he filled Kyle's mind with nothing but force and power. Kyle was brought up like that and he's not going to change. He was with the old man for over fourteen years and it's all too deeply ingrained. He takes what he wants.'

'When Kyle comes home tonight——' Alexandra began but she got no further.

'I'm sorry, my dear, but he won't be home, not tonight. He seems to have a deep craving for me at the moment. Maybe you should have given in? But then,' she added, looking at Alexandra sympathetically, 'if you had, you wouldn't be here now in this house. It would all be over and Kyle would be on his way, which is what he'll do long before you get to the altar.'

'There's not too long before this weekend,' Alexandra said firmly, 'and all this is none of your business.'

Dulcie stood and picked up her bag. 'There will be delays, unavoidable delays, and in the meantime he'll pressurise you. I've seen it all before, as I say. The moment you give in, the wedding will be off. I only came to warn you, my dear. You're quite young, something utterly new for Kyle, I suspect.'

She wouldn't believe it, she wouldn't! Her mind was treacherously going over her knowledge of Kyle, the time he spent with that woman, his cold determination to get exactly what he wanted—but he needed her and she was clinging to her dreams as if her life depended on it. It did at that moment, because Kyle already owned her and only time would tell if he really intended to marry her. She felt treacherous but she knew Kyle's ways. Wasn't it because Kyle never bowed to defeat that she was here in the first place?

Alexandra was still standing, white-faced and shivering, when Graves came to the door. 'Telephone, Miss Alexandra. Mr Maddison.'

She flew to the phone, desperate to tell Kyle about the visit and desperate to hear his caustic comments on Dulcie Hepworth. She never got the chance.

'Alex,' he said straight away. 'I've just left Steven and he'll tell you all about our meeting this afternoon. I may be in very late—in fact I'll probably not be in at all. I'll see you tomorrow.'

He was staying with Dulcie tonight. It was all true. She did not answer and his voice sharpened with something like anxiety.

'Alex?'

'I—I heard you,' she said shakily. 'I'll see you tomorrow, then.'

'What's wrong?' he asked tersely, hearing her tremors even over the telephone, and she lied quickly, an excuse right at the top of her mind.

'My headache,' she murmured. 'I—I think it's coming back.'

'Oh, Alex. I wish I were there,' he said softly and deeply. 'I didn't want to leave you this morning. I can't come back, though. Go to bed and let Graves fix you something.'

She was glad he wasn't there, glad he couldn't see her dreams unravelling, and when he ended the call she stood looking at the telephone as if it was an enemy. He had confirmed everything. He was going to Dulcie tonight—

again. Even after last night . . . She had done well to tell herself that she was mad, because now that she had belonged to him he was satisfied, his obsession over. She wouldn't wait for the excuses. She couldn't!

It took her very little time to pack and she didn't give any thought as to how she was going to get to the station. Steven had taken a taxi—so would she. She counted out her money and she had enough for a taxi at both ends of her journey and enough for the train. She took off her engagement ring and put it carefully on the dressing-table where Kyle would find it. She put the pearls with it, the leather box closed. It all looked so final, but then, it was.

Before Graves realised what she was doing she had her cases in the hall, a taxi coming up the drive, and the old man looked stricken.

'Miss Alexandra! You can't seriously be leaving! You must be ill again.' He sounded shocked and she felt a surge of sympathy for him.

'I'm not ill, Graves. Not any more.'

She shook hands with him and went out to the taxi, telling herself that this was freedom but knowing that it was a road to despair. What would Kyle do about Steven now? She couldn't let that influence her—she had allowed it to too much already and this time she had to get away for good. Last night had tied her to Kyle forever but it had not tied him to her. It was all part of the plan; first the shares, and lastly, her.

She couldn't help turning for one last look at the house, though, and Graves was standing on the step, his whole figure dejected as if he had failed Kyle finally. She turned away, her face tight with control. There would be someone else there soon, or Dulcie. Graves knew Dulcie, so it was quite clear that she had been more than once. She had probably slept there plenty of times.

Her hands clenched, her nails digging into her soft skin as she stifled the cry that rose to her lips. She would get over it. Steven would get over it. They had been perfectly all right until Kyle had come along. She was too honest to go on telling herself that, though. They had not been perfectly all right and she had not been happy; neither had Steven.

'Oh, Kyle.' She whispered his name in despair and the driver looked at her through the rear-view mirror.

'Did you say something, miss?'

'Nothing at all,' she said wearily.

Mrs Nash was there as soon as Alexandra arrived in another taxi from the station. It was just getting dark but Mrs Nash had eyes like a hawk if she was on the hunt for gossip. 'Well, you're coming back, Alexandra?' she asked brightly, her eyes everywhere.

'I'm coming to clean the house,' Alexandra said quickly, ignoring the inquisitive eyes that went to her suitcases. She bent to lift them and the same eyes darted to her fingers.

'That lovely ring. I saw it in the papers when you got engaged. I hope you haven't lost it?'

'No. It's not the thing to wear for cleaning a house, Mrs Nash. It's too expensive.'

It began to rain and she grasped the excuse to get away, hurrying inside and closing the door. How long could she keep up the pretence? How long could she hide from herself and everyone else? She left her cases by the door and walked into the sitting-room. It was so dull, so cold, so lonely, not her home any more. She bent down and lit a fire, getting more coal and occupying herself with that for several minutes. What she was going to do to occupy the rest of her life she didn't know. One minute at a time while it lasts, that was what Kyle had said.

She began to use the minutes, getting her jeans on and a soft shirt, tying her hair back and starting the cleaning she had not come to do. She kept the fire going too, stoking it as if she were doomed should it go out. It was something to keep an eye on, something else to think about, and the rain poured down outside like tears as the night became dark.

Alexandra was cleaning the kitchen at eight o'clock, her arms hurting, her head aching, and she knew perfectly well that this was all wrong. It was not many days since she had been quite ill after her accident. She rested her head for a minute, closing her eyes, jumping and screaming when hard hands grasped her.

'What the hell are you doing?' Kyle spun her round, his eyes blazing with temper. 'Yes, I used Steven's key again! And yes, I've come to get you!' he roared. His hair was wet and he was wearing a trench coat, open over his suit. The coat was wet at the shoulders too and she couldn't seem to think of anything else.

'Alex!' He was explosive. She had never seen him so angry before and she just blurted out the thing at the top of her mind.

'I'm not marrying you, Kyle, and I'm not ever coming back.'

He let her go and stared down at her and she brushed past him, going into the sitting-room to stand looking at the fire, anything to keep her from looking at Kyle.

'Explain.' He had followed her in and stood in the doorway making the room seem tiny, his face set and hard.

'I've come to my senses, that's all. You've pressurised me from the first, Kyle, making plans that included me whether I wanted them or not, threatening me about Steven. It's all over, though. You were right when you said that Steven had grown up. I realised that today. For the first time he'll have to face the consequences of his actions and I can't do anything at all to help because it would mean giving up my life, and I've only got the one life.'

She knew she was babbling on but it seemed impossible to stop and he just stared at her with those grey eyes until she wanted to hide away.

'And marrying me would be wasting it,' he finished for her in a curiously flat voice. She wouldn't answer that.

'If you decide to—to send Steven back to that woman at the court and let him f-face that, then you'll just have to do it. I can't be bullied or forced into anything any more.'

'He's not going back there,' Kyle said tightly. 'I don't put a lot of work into things to simply let them slide away.'

'Only with me,' Alexandra assured him shakily. 'I'm sliding away because I just can't face things any more. You're wasting your time again, Kyle, coming here. You might just as well go to Dulcie—where you intended to be tonight.'

'You have a lot of trust in me, don't you?' he grated bitterly. 'I know she came—Graves told me. I was flying to Scotland tonight, with Ian, but I cancelled it and came back as soon as I could when I heard how you sounded. It doesn't matter. You don't have to face anything else. I know when to cut my losses. Don't worry about Steven. He can come back here or stay with me, as he chooses. I think he's old enough to choose now. I'm not pressurising you, Alex. I noticed the ring. You're free.'

It was everything she had intended but the words hit her deep inside so hard that she almost cried out. She didn't, though. She kept her face still, and in any case he was not looking at her. He put his hands in his pockets, pushing his wet coat back, and walked to the window where the curtains were still open. The rain was driving against the lights of the street lamps, dashing in the dark grey pools of water that had collected. It looked cold and unhappy, so very fitting for this night.

Alexandra looked at him, at the broad shoulders and the dark hair that tended to curl around his nape, her hands wanting to touch him but her mind telling her that this was how it should end, with Kyle's silence and her own. She realised that she knew him well after all. In a moment he would turn and go without a word, hard and silent as he was in everything.

'You don't need me, Kyle,' she said with soft bitterness, unable to maintain the silence. 'You—you have this special arrangement with Dulcie Hepwarth and——'

'That's right,' he bit out harshly. 'We have a very special arrangement. She chases me and I ignore her. Don't hide behind Dulcie, at least she doesn't pretend. With her it's an open pursuit of money—my money. The truth will do just fine, Alex. You hated me on sight and I tricked and bullied you. I also scared you to death. Smoke-screens are unnecessary between you and me. You're free. I told you that.'

He was silent again, but only for a moment and then he drove his fist into the wall hard enough to really hurt. 'Lord, how will I manage?' he said hoarsely. 'I love you so much, Alex.'

Small, poisonous words came into her mind, words that Dulcie had said, that he would use other tricks, but her mind refused to accept them. He looked forlorn, alone, as dark and lonely as the night outside, as dark and lonely as she had felt.

She walked across, her footsteps silent on the carpet, and her arms wound around him, her face against the wet material of his coat. She couldn't say anything and when he turned slowly and took her shoulders in hands that trembled she looked up into his eyes.

'Are you mothering me, Alex?'

Even his voice trembled, and she shook her head, her hands coming to cup his face as she stood on tiptoe and lifted her lips for him. 'No. I'm loving you, Kyle. At least let me do that even if we're free of each other.'

'Alex!' He pulled her into his arms and rocked her, holding her tightly, his face against her hair. 'Free? I'll never be free. I'll see your face in front of me for the rest of my life, feel you in my arms always.'

'That's where I want to be,' she begged, her eyes filling with tears. 'I love you, Kyle. Don't set me free either.'

His lips covered hers urgently, almost desperately, and she clung to him with joy soaring inside her. He really loved her. All the harsh desperation told her that. She was home again, back in Kyle's arms.

'Darling, I'm making you all wet,' he said shakily after a while, and she laughed against him, her cheeks already wet with the tears that poured down.

'I don't care. I don't care,' she sobbed.

'Don't cry, sweetheart. Please don't cry,' he begged distractedly. He looked down at her as if he didn't know what to do, his powerful world unbalanced for the first time. 'Your headache. You've been working here, cleaning. I've got to look after you better. You've got to let me!'

'I only want you to love me, Kyle. Everything else will take care of itself.'

He lifted her face then, his eyes moving over her tear-wet cheeks, and he pulled the band from her hair, letting it swing free and stroking it back from her face. 'Don't tie it back,' he whispered. 'I like to see it like this, all around your face. I used to watch you when you stayed at night. I could see your hair shining in the lights and I wanted to touch it, to touch you, but you were so far away from me, so distant.'

He pulled off his coat and jacket, dropping them in a chair, and moved her back into his arms, looking down at her and then burying his face against her neck. 'Can I touch you now, Alex darling? Are you mine? If you leave me . . .'

'I'll never leave you, Kyle.' She wound her arms around his neck. 'I thought you didn't love me, and wanting isn't enough.'

'No, it isn't,' he agreed softly, some of the dreadful tension easing from him. 'I thought it would have to be. I thought you would never love me, but I couldn't let you go. Not until I heard you tonight. Then I knew I couldn't force you to be with me.'

'You're not forcing me now, and I'm right here,' she said softly, and for the first time his eyes began to smile, his hands began to stroke her as she nestled against him.

The telephone rang and Alex reached out and picked it up, distracted by the kisses that Kyle rained on her wet cheeks and her slender neck. 'H-hello?' she managed, and Steven's voice came very loud and clear, clear enough for Kyle to hear because they were tightly in each other's arms.

'Alex? What the devil are you up to now? It's too bad, Alex, you used to behave like a perfectly normal person and nowadays it's impossible to know what you'll do next. I got home to find Graves looking like death, almost in tears. He said Kyle had torn out of the house like a madman. How are we going to find him, Alex? He'll probably have an accident and small wonder, the way you behave!'

Kyle took the phone from her hand as she stood open-mouthed listening to her baby brother telling her off. 'I'm here,' he said quietly, a grin stretched across his face, 'and Alex is behaving very well indeed. We'll exchange all our news when we get together—tomorrow.'

Steven went on talking but Alex wasn't listening; she was nestling against Kyle, her face burrowing against his warmth, and when he put the phone down and tilted her face she suddenly felt shy.

'What was he saying?' she asked winsomely, and Kyle looked down at her with smiling eyes.

'He was suggesting that I put you across my knee and administer some discipline,' he told her, laughing when she looked outraged. 'I have other plans, though, but I'll not tell Steven tomorrow.'

'Tomorrow?' she asked tremulously.

'Let's stay here tonight, Alex. Just you and me. Let's sit by this great roaring fire and talk.'

He didn't wait for any answer. He led her to the settee and sat down beside her, pulling her into his arms, his face against her hair as she looked into the flames that were dancing like her own heart. She just lay against him, saying nothing at all, her hand in his, not wanting the moment to end, and he sighed against her hair.

'I can't believe it. Is it true, darling? Do you love me?'

'I love you, Kyle,' she said softly, looking up at him, knowing he needed to hear it many times. 'I've loved you for a long time, before I even knew it myself. The first time I saw you something happened inside me and it just grew no matter how angry I was, no matter how hurt——'

'Don't!' He kissed her lips with a deep tenderness. 'I didn't want to hurt you but I couldn't just go away and leave you. I loved you from the first moment I saw you and the next day, when you were standing in that foyer, looking at me as if I were some sort of visiting devil, I knew I had to have you for myself somehow.'

She began to laugh. 'I wondered if you were a visiting devil. I'd placed such high hopes on you, the Wonder Man, and then you scared me at the restaurant and when you came in next day, looking so powerful and for-bidding, I was sort of panic-stricken.'

'So was I,' he confessed ruefully, 'because I was facing something I'd never faced in my life and I wasn't sure how to cope.'

'You could have tried telling me,' Alexandra said severely, looking up at him, and he grinned wryly.

'By the time I was close enough to risk telling you I was too deep in my own plots to get out of them.' He sighed and cuddled her close. 'You were quite right—I only wanted the land. Fosdick-Kent is standing on a gold mine, the land far more valuable than the firm. It's perfect for a super hotel complex. But when I saw you there was no way I was going to wind the firm up and get rid of the staff. I needed you as I've never needed anyone in my life. Every plan I made since then has been with you in mind.'

'Including rescuing Steven and capturing me,' Alex pointed out quietly.

'I didn't do that to capture you initially,' he confessed softly. 'I saw your face all white and strained and I knew you had problems. I already knew about Steven. I went to a lot of trouble to find out all about you. When I saw you in that court with that hard-faced lady glaring at you I could have killed Steven. I wanted to scoop you up and walk out with you. The only way I could do it was the way I did.' He kissed the top of her head as she gazed into the fire. 'When I saw you in my house I wanted to keep you there in any way I could.'

'Including ruining my reputation?'

He held her tightly, tilting her face to his, his eyes regretful. 'Try to understand me, Alex, darling,' he begged. 'I'm a creature of long conditioning, my life built on planning and being one jump ahead. The two people I loved most in the world left me and I was never going to love again because it hurt too much. My grand-father showed me how to avoid all hurt. When I wanted something I just went after it, all senses alert. It was the only way I knew to get you. When you were hurt by all the gossip I had to do something about it.'

'You started it in the first place by saying I was living with you,' Alexandra complained, looking up at him severely, and his cheekbones flared with colour

'I was dreaming aloud,' he said with an embarrassed look that had her laughing and reaching up to kiss him.

'Kyle, darling, you can dream. Even the strongest people dream. It doesn't make you abnormal.'

'It's the only dream I've ever allowed myself,' he confessed, his lip searching for hers. 'Oh, Alex. I thought you were in love with Davis and he's such a wimp.'

'He's nothing of the sort!' Alexandra protested, pulling back. 'He's a very nice, quiet person.'

'All right, then, he's a very nice wimp.' Kyle laughed, lifting her on to his knee. 'I thought you were so annoyed at being kept late because you were missing him, and I was keeping you late so that you couldn't see him— and so that I could see you,' he added ruefully. 'It was almost childish and I was ashamed of myself when you began to look so tired.'

Alexandra leaned back on his arm and looked into his eyes. She had one worry, and he had said nothing at all about it. 'When you stayed out late, when I was at your house, I—I thought you were with Dulcie.'

He grimaced. 'I was keeping away from you, sheer self-defence. My own feelings were getting out of control.'

'She told me that she was in America with you, that you went there for one of her shows.'

'I did not!' he assured her angrily, turning her face to his. 'Surely you know she'll say anything at all to get her own way.'

'She knew all about your grandfather.'

'So does half the world,' he snorted. 'As your Aunt Cora said so truthfully, I'm always in the papers. Don't keep on about Dulcie, Alex. She's a pain.'

'The phone calls at your house when I first came didn't sound like that,' Alexandra said hotly.

'You were there,' he reminded her with a sudden grin. 'I had to take action to protect myself even at that stage. It made a lot of trouble, though,' he grumbled. 'She thought I meant it.'

'Serves you right,' Alexandra said firmly.

'You're jealous. It's wonderful,' Kyle said, lifting her face, and she looked sadly at him.

'It's not wonderful. It hurts.'

'Nothing is going to hurt you again,' he said softly, cradling her against him. 'I love you and I'm going to make life wonderful for all of us.'

They stayed wrapped in each other's arms, sometimes talking, sometimes simply looking at the fire, and Alexandra had never felt so contented, so happy.

'You're tired,' Kyle said gently later, as words died between them and the fire became a soft red glow. 'Go to bed, Alex, and I'll stay here all night. This is a comfortable settee.'

'I won't leave you.' She sat up and put her arms around him, surprised to see his face filled with tension.

'At the end of the week we'll be married,' he said softly, suddenly burying his face against her. 'I've caused you a lot of grief and a lot of hurt, darling. I'm not going to sleep with you tonight. I'll show you that I love you and that it isn't just wanting.'

'Don't you want me now?' Alexandra asked, her lips trailing across his face as he looked up at her.

'Oh, lord, Alex. I never stop wanting you. Wherever you are, whatever you're doing, even when you were ill and in pain...'

'When I lived here,' she whispered blushingly, 'I had a bed. I expect it's still there.'

'Alex! Don't torture me!' His grey eyes filled with agony and she wound her arms around his neck, hiding her face against him.

'But you're torturing me, Kyle. I don't want to close my eyes if you're not there. I don't want to do that any more.'

He gasped at the sweet plaintive sound of her voice and tilted her face to his, looking into her eyes for a long time before he spoke. 'I love you,' he said deeply. 'I swore never to place my life in any other hands but my own, but you've placed your life in my hands. The world is a changed place for me.'

'And for me. It changed the moment I saw you, Kyle,' Alexandra said softly. 'I once thought that even if it was a dream and I woke up and found you didn't really exist I would never get over it.'

His face softened magically and he lifted her into his arms and stood. 'I adore you, Alexandra Kent,' he murmured against her lips, 'and I'm going to show you how much.'

The room was warm when they went upstairs and the curtains were drawn against the rainy night. As Kyle gently undressed her she could hear the steady dripping of rain from the eaves and suddenly it was the most comforting sound in the world. He looked down at her and she smiled, her arms lifting to cling to him as he undressed.

'Do I still frighten you, sweetheart?' he asked quietly. 'I know I have done in the past. I wanted you so much that it just all boiled over, like a rage that I couldn't control. Deep inside I never thought you'd come to me of your own free will and I also knew that I could never manage to go on as normal without you. I know I hurt you.'

'I was scared,' she confessed. 'Mostly, though, it was because I had never felt so strongly about anyone, never felt myself swept away with no hope of recovery. I wanted to drown in you and I thought——'

'Drown in me now, Alex,' he begged, coming to her and taking her in his arms. 'I've been waiting for you all my life.'

Their feelings were too heated for words, their lips unwilling to be parted, and she felt his blaze of passion as she melted into him, her hands as eager to touch him as his were to touch her. He covered her with kisses, his fingers coaxing and caressing, and her soft moans as she twisted beneath him seemed to light a fire in them both.

His kisses became fierce, his body pressed tightly to hers, his skin burning. 'I need you, Alex,' he groaned huskily. 'We'll be like this every night all our lives but I'll never have enough of you, never stop wanting you. It pulls me apart.'

She wound herself around him, soft and willing, her breathing as uneven as his own, and he possessed her fiercely, all thought of control gone, her wild little cry like a signal to him.

'Alex! Oh, Alex,' he murmured against her skin, his hands running over her proprietorially when they finally returned to earth and she gave a long, shaken sigh.

'I really belong to you now,' she whispered. 'This time it was different because we've spoken the truth, we know each other. Did I disappoint you, Kyle? Do you still love me?'

'My love, my love,' he moaned, his lips covering hers for trembling minutes, his own eyes suspiciously damp.

Later, as he moved and she curled up to him, her head on his shoulder, he stroked her satin-smooth body, his hands still not too steady. He couldn't seem to speak and, when her voice came softly into the lamplit room, she said something he would never have imaged.

'I'm sorry now that I gave your flowers away.'

He smiled, tightening his arms around her, shaking his head in amused disbelief. He never knew what she was going to say or do next. 'Why did you, then?'

'I thought that you'd just sent those because it was the right thing to do.' She looked up at him with soft dark eyes. 'The private room, the red roses, everything all arranged nicely for the fiancée of Kyle Maddison.'

'The private room was because I didn't know any other way of making you safe and comfortable,' he said. He smiled ruefully. 'The roses? Well, I wanted to just send you one, with all my love, but I didn't have the nerve.'

'All you wrote on the card was your name,' she complained, and he looked down at her wryly.

'After ruining about six cards because I didn't know how much I dare put. The woman at the shop was getting a bit stroppy by then. You kept Davis' flowers,' he added in a grieved voice.

'But they were ordinary, Kyle. Something I could cope with. I'm not used to being treated like a queen.'

'It will grow on you,' he said drily. 'Unless of course I decide to follow you around all the time and let the Maddison Group go damn. Not that Ian would allow it,' he added. 'I wonder how he's going on in Scotland?'

'Why were you going there?'

'A hotel. There's a big country mansion outside Edinburgh. The owner is willing to sell, but he refuses to cross the border. We were going up to clinch the deal but I was sidetracked by a runaway fiancée. Ian went alone.'

'Oh, I'm sorry,' Alexandra said contritely, but he laughed softly and lifted her face.

'Are you?' he asked seductively, turning towards her. 'Any other prying you have to do before we get to other matters?'

'I always wondered what Carruthers' first name was,' she said quickly, her face flushed and her eyes bright.

'Bill,' he informed her, his glance amused and sensuous all at the same time.

'How disappointing. It's just an ordinary name. I thought he was a mathematical genius.'

'So he is,' Kyle murmured as he moved closer and tightened her against him. 'A very ordinary mathematical genius. What else do you want to know?'

Alexandra never answered because as she opened her mouth he captured it, and she was soon too lost in love to ask any other questions.

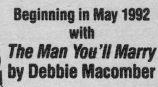

FREE GIFT OFFER

To receive your free gift, send us the specified number of proofs-of-purchase from any specially marked Free Gift Offer Harlequin or Silhouette book with the Free Gift Certificate properly completed, plus a check or money order (do not send cash) to cover postage and handling payable to Harlequin/Silhouette Free Gift Promotion Offer. We will send you the specified gift.

FREE GIFT CERTIFICATE

ITEM	A. GOLD TONE EARRINGS	B. GOLD TONE BRACELET	C. GOLD TONE NECKLACE
# of proofs-of-purchase required	3	6	9
Postage and Handling	$1.75	$2.25	$2.75
Check one	☐	☐	☐

Name: _____

Address: _____

City: _____ State: _____ Zip Code: _____

Mail this certificate, specified number of proofs-of-purchase and a check or money order for postage and handling to: HARLEQUIN/SILHOUETTE FREE GIFT OFFER 1992, P.O. Box 9057, Buffalo, NY 14269-9057. Requests must be received by July 31, 1992.

PLUS—Every time you submit a completed certificate with the correct number of proofs-of-purchase, you are automatically entered in our MILLION DOLLAR SWEEPSTAKES! No purchase or obligation necessary to enter. See below for alternate means of entry and how to obtain complete sweepstakes rules.

MILLION DOLLAR SWEEPSTAKES
NO PURCHASE OR OBLIGATION NECESSARY TO ENTER

To enter, hand-print (mechanical reproductions are not acceptable) your name and address on a 3″×5″ card and mail to Million Dollar Sweepstakes 6097, c/o either P.O. Box 9056, Buffalo, NY 14269-9056 or P.O. Box 621, Fort Erie, Ontario L2A 5X3. Limit: one entry per envelope. Entries must be sent via 1st-class mail. For eligibility, entries must be received no later than March 31, 1994. No liability is assumed for printing errors, lost, late or misdirected entries.

Sweepstakes is open to persons 18 years of age or older. All applicable laws and regulations apply. Sweepstakes offer void wherever prohibited by law. Prizewinners will be determined no later than May 1994. Chances of winning are determined by the number of entries distributed and received. For a copy of the Official Rules governing this sweepstakes offer, send a self-addressed, stamped envelope (WA residents need not affix return postage) to: Million Dollar Sweepstakes Rules, P.O. Box 4733, Blair, NE 68009.

HP1U

ONE PROOF-OF-PURCHASE
To collect your fabulous FREE GIFT you must include the necessary FREE GIFT proofs-of-purchase with a properly completed offer certificate.

(See center insert for details)

TASTY FOOD COMPETITION

Reading Harlequin romances may win you a valuable prize! Here's how: when you complete the word search game below and return it to us by May 31, 1992, we will enter your name in a draw for a fabulous Old-Time Radio. The Collector's Edition Radio, by Philco, is a faithful reproduction of a 1938 classic. It combines the classic design of the original with state-of-the-art play capability (AM/FM and Cassette), in a beautiful wood-grain finish. The first 10 properly completed entries chosen by random draw will receive one FREE, just for entering the Harlequin Tasty Food Competition.

H	O	L	L	A	N	D	A	I	S	E	R
E	Y	E	G	G	O	W	H	A	O	H	A
R	S	E	E	C	L	A	I	R	U	C	T
B	T	K	K	A	E	T	S	I	F	I	A
E	E	T	I	S	M	A	L	C	F	U	T
U	R	C	M	T	L	H	E	E	L	Q	O
G	S	I	U	T	F	O	N	O	E	D	U
N	H	L	S	O	T	O	N	E	F	M	I
I	S	R	S	O	M	A	C	W	A	A	L
R	I	A	E	E	T	I	R	J	A	E	L
E	F	G	L	L	P	T	O	T	V	R	E
M	O	U	S	S	E	E	O	D	O	C	P

CLAM	GARLIC	MELON	PRAWN	SALT
COD	HERB	MERINGUE	QUICHE	SOUFFLE
CREAM	HOLLANDAISE	MOUSSE	RATATOUILLE	SPICE
ECLAIR	JAM	MUSSELS	RICE	STEAK
EGG	LEEK	OYSTERS	RISOTTO	TART
FISH	LEMON			

Please turn over for entry details

HOW TO ENTER

All the words listed are hidden in the word puzzle grid. You can find them by reading the letters forward, backward, up and down, or diagonally. When you find a word, circle it or put a line through it. Then fill in your name and address in the space provided, put this page in an envelope and mail it today to:

Harlequin Word Search Contest
Harlequin Reader Service®
P.O. Box 9071
Buffalo, NY 14269-9071

NEXT MONTH:
YOU COULD GET A FREE
GE SPACEMAKER TV!
STAY TUNED!

NAME _____

ADDRESS _____

_____

CITY _____ STATE _____ ZIP CODE _____

H2APR2